SONNY'S BOY

Book Three of the Twin Flames Trilogy

SPENCER MICHAELS

Evatopia Editions

Contents

Acknowledgement

A special thanks to Pastor Jimmy Calhoun for his contribution to the apologetics used in Chapter 23.

Publisher's Cataloging-In-Publication Data
(Prepared by The Donohue Group, Inc.)
Names: Michaels, Spencer.
Title: Sonny's boy / Spencer Michaels.
Description: [Beverly Hills, California] : Evatopia Editions, [2018] | Series: [Twin flames trilogy] ; [book 3]
Identifiers: ISBN 9781630991272 (paperback) | ISBN 9781630991258 (ePub) | ISBN 9781630991265 (mobi)
Subjects: LCSH: Clairvoyants--Fiction. | Families--Fiction. | Animals, Mythical--Fiction. | Man-woman relationships--Fiction. | Good and evil--Fiction. | LCGFT: Fantasy fiction.
Classification: LCC PS3613.I34 S65 2018 (print) | LCC PS3613.I34 (ebook) | DDC 813/.6--dc23

Chapter One

*L*ight always shines greyest when you can't seem to make sense of the world, when what you're seeing just can't be true.

I sat on the front steps of Big Guy's home in New Bern after attending his funeral. I kept running the coin necklace that Marty had given me through my fingers, looking for answers to pour forth from it. Was this the actual mysterious coin necklace that Big Guy had talked about? And what kind of cryptic bullshit was that that Marty had told me? Why give this to my firstborn grandson? I'm not even married for Christ's sake. And what did he mean by he'd see me then? Am I going to die as soon as I have a grand-child? What the fuck? And most importantly, why hadn't Big Guy let me in on the *great escape?*

Marty came out, Blue Moon in hand, and sat down beside me.

After a few minutes of silence, Marty burped and said, "Hey Sonny, did I ever tell you about how your grandfather and Nan finally got together?"

"No Marty, but Big Guy sorta did. I was helping him write down his memoirs...well, what he could remember. I'm sure some of that crazy shit he told me wasn't true, but he gave me a lot of fond memories of him trying to retell the stories of his life. He was trying to write a book. I promised I would help him compile it as he just wasn't getting anywhere trying to put it down on paper. You know how he was...everything had to be just right, so he never got past the first paragraph."

"Now, that's funny. The old shit writing a book. Was I in it?"

"Oh, yeah..."

"Well, whatever he put in it about me was probably a pack of lies."

"Maybe so, maybe so."

Marty swirled the beer around in his bottle trying to find some words to comfort Sonny. He sighed a deep sigh and took then another sip of beer.

"You know, some of that crazy shit he told you about in the book...it may not be as crazy as you think. Mark and Sopie were some very unique people. They weren't like the rest of us. There was something way different in the way they did things and the way they saw things. They also were courageous individuals, who did things that combat veterans would shun."

"What do you mean, Marty?"

"Well, I really don't know all of the details, but I can tell you that I am glad that I was never on the enemy side of the wall. I did have a chance to see the old man in action once."

Taking another sip of beer, he continued, "Mark was around fifty then, when the two of us decided to go to Willie Mae's Scotch House in Treme for some fried chicken, red beans and rice. We left, and it was getting dark as we walked to our car. I never saw them, but three guys came up behind us and were planning to mug us. Next thing I know, this old, supposedly crippled friend of mine, who walks with a cane, beat the ever loving shit out of the three of them, one with a knife, and knocks them unconscious. Then, instead of jumping in our car and getting the hell out of there, he goes and revives all three, who then take off running. He said it would hurt his Karma or some shit if he left them there to suffer."

"Wait...are you shitting me? That's the same story that Big Guy told me...it's true?"

"Cross my heart. I was there; I saw it. Well, I saw something. The whole fight was probably ten seconds long."

"Seven...Big Guy said it was seven."

"Old fuck. Only he would count." And they both laughed.

"Uncle Marty, why do you really suppose he insisted that you give me this necklace?" Sonny asked, as he again rolled it through his fingers.

"I'm not sure, but he was adamant about me giving it to you and what he told me to tell you, word for word, about it. I knew him better than anyone except maybe your Nan and she, God love her, had to put up with both of our sorry asses. But I can tell you one thing for sure, if that stubborn old coot was that damn serious about wanting something done in a certain way, that's the way he meant for it to be done. If he said to make sure that you give that to your first grandson, then, by God, that is what he meant for you to do...and you better do it."

Laughing, I said, "I don't even have a wife yet or any children."

Marty said, "Look, I told you that I knew him and Sopie for a long time. I don't know how, but they had a grasp on what was to be. Put it in the back of your mind for now, but don't be surprised at how things turn out. Shit...I gotta piss and get a drink. Be back in a few. You need anything?"

"No, I'm good."

Just as I had settled back into my thoughts, Dad came out and leaned on the front porch post with two glasses in hand.

"Hi, Dad. You doing okay?"

"Yeah, I'm fine. I brought us two scotches to give a private toast to Dad."

"He would have liked that," I said standing, giving Dad a hug, "What is it?"

"The rest of the Yamazaki 21. He only served it to his honored guests, and I suppose we are the last of them," Dad said tearing up.

"It only seems right," I said, taking my glass.

We held the glasses up and sipped the liquor savoring, not only the nectar but the memories of the man we once knew and loved so much.

"You know Dad, I was just out here with Uncle Marty, and I was telling him about me helping Big Guy write his memoirs, and I told him that some of the stories were really unbelievable. So, he begins to tell me a story about him and Big Guy in New Orleans, where Big Guy whipped some serious ass...and it confirmed one of the stories that Big Guy had told me. I guess I just never thought of Big Guy as being such a badass."

"Well, he was a man of many surprises. He was a just and caring human being with an unbelievable sense of humor. He would try to make you think he was a drunk all of the time, but I never saw the man soused. He and Mom would go round and round about his drinking, but it was really a joke. He enjoyed his scotch very much, as you know, and he was quite the connoisseur."

"But what about all those stories he told me about Master Bennie. Surely that couldn't be for real."

"Well, I don't know what he told you, but Master Bennie was very much real. They even baked a cake together."

"Baked a cake!"

"Long story...another day. I will say this, from what I understand, Master Bennie sorta took Mark under his wing when he lived in Los Angeles. After Dad's car accident that left him a cripple, Master Bennie taught him how to rebuild his life. He also taught him a lot of other things that I never fully understood, but I never really understood the things that Mom was able to do either."

"What do you mean? What could Nan do?"

"Well, Mom was a psychic, but she was a lot more than that. From what I can gather through conversations they had after they moved back down here, she could move objects by willing them, and she also could travel through portals that transcended time and space...I know, it sounds like Sci-Fi, but I walked in one day while she was cleaning and she had the broom sweeping and the mop mopping without holding them. Yeah, freaky family."

"I am beginning to see that."

"Well, they never talked much about it, but I think the real reason that they moved back down here from Canada was that they had to do something courageous, that saved the town that they lived in from a calamity. However, the residents were so disturbed by the powers they used to accomplish whatever it was they did, that the townspeople and the villagers became scared to the point that the council bought them out so they would move."

"I think F.P., when he was living, knew but he wouldn't say much about it, other than he was glad to go fishin' with his buddy down here."

"I've always wondered, why did they call him F.P.?"

Laughing, Dad just said, "Don't ask."

"Well, I had no idea about this. I just dismissed Big Guy's stories as to him being delusional. So, Nan was a badass, too?"

"More than you could ever know. She was the sweetest woman that ever walked on the face of this earth, but you know the reason Big Guy got so upset before her funeral is that she used a portal to save him, knowing it would cause her death. That's just the way she was. My mom cared for me and protected me when nobody else could, even when it would mean turning from the love of her life to ensure my safety. Mom was definitely a different kind of hero. I guess Big Guy just could never forgive himself. I think he just let himself slip away since Mom died. I also believe his memory lapses were his body's way of protecting him from the thoughts he just could not handle. Say, why don't we go in. It's getting a little chilly out here for me."

"You go ahead, Dad. I think I'll just sit out here a little while longer."

Again, I was deep in reflection, and again my reverie was broken by the opening of the screen door.

"Hello, Mister. I was wondering where you had gotten off to," said Amy as she plopped down next to me. It was that comfortable and familiar type of plop that she used to do down at the marina.

Billy and Elva Miller, her parents, came to the funeral but decided to go home afterward. It had been a long day for everyone. I was surprised by the number of people that had attended the funeral. It was not as big a crowd as had shown up for Nan's, but it was still a huge crowd. Even Sally "Cock Rockets," as Big Guy used to call her, was in attendance. John, the orderly that he had derided for all those years, was there with tears in his eyes. I think he, above all others, really understood the old man and why he was the way he was.

"Well hello, Sunshine," I said. "Finally came out to brighten my day?"

"Absolutely!" said Amy. "Just like I would on any other day."

"That's an affirmative. So...when do you head back to Galveston?"

"In a couple of days. Then I've got to make my moving plans, and I should be back in about a month."

"Back? You're moving back here?"

"Yes, silly. I told you that a while ago. A position opened up at the UNC Institute for Marine Sciences, and I applied and got the job. So, I will be back for good after next month. Do you think you can live without me for that long?"

"Well, I have been getting along pretty nicely without you so far," I retorted.

"I didn't say get along; I said *LIVE*! Neither of our lives has been too much outside of our work. I think it's time to change that."

"And by changing that, you mean changing me?"

"If you are up for it, old man," she said tickling him playfully.

"STOP! You have always been the pushy one."

"Me, pushy? How did you get that idea, Sonny?"

"I wonder," I said. "Okay, tell you what. Let's blow this joint and get a drink at the Beach Tavern, sorta in honor of Big Guy."

"Whoa, that's 45 minutes away. Do you think we can get back without getting a DUI?"

"Sure, I got it covered. Come on chicken, shit or get off the pot."

"Alright Bucko, you gotta deal."

"No, I gotta date!"

"Yes, you do," she said kissing me gently on the cheek. "You better go tell Vinnie and Angel where we are off to so they won't worry."

"I suppose I should. I feel like I am seventeen again, going to the prom."

"As you should, Mister," said Amy. "Hurry back."

I rushed inside to grab a jacket and to bid everyone goodbye, then went back out to meet Amy.

"Mom said she would call Billy and Elva to let them know where we are heading so they won't have to worry, either."

"Your mom and dad are so thoughtful. I can't imagine why any of them would worry about me when I am out with you...Oh yeah, the boat thing..."

"Yeah, the boat thing..." I said laughing as we headed toward Atlantic Beach.

Chapter Two

*F*inally arriving at Atlantic Beach, we turned right heading down Salterpath to our destination. Big Guy used to call this *The Happiest Place on Earth,* but when we arrived there were only half a dozen cars in the parking lot. We went in to find four old codgers at the bar. We took our places on the stools, and the beertender (because you didn't want anything else) said, "What'll y'all have?"

"Blue Moons?" I said hesitantly.

"Okay, right wit'cha. Here you go," he said as two bottles were presented.

Amy said, "Nothing but the best for my dog!"

"Easy girl, easy," I said looking around nervously.

We swilled the brews to gather our courage and ordered a couple of more rounds that were quickly devoured. Suddenly, Amy jumped up grabbing me by the hand.

"Hey look! A real jukebox with records. Let's see if they have any beach tunes on it."

We found an old Embers song called, *I Love Beach Music.*

"Can you shag?" asked Amy.

"Of course, I can."

"Let's go, then," she said as she pulled me onto the floor.

We danced and drank and danced and yeah...drank...a lot. One of the old guys then got up to play a song on the jukebox.

"I figured you kids would like a slow one. It's a good old song from the seventies. I think you'll like it. One of my favorites from a guy that, I hear, used to play at the beach down here."

And the song began. And Amy and I danced...close...very close with Amy rubbing up against me. As she looked up, her eyes glistened from the lights shining behind them. My heart was melting. It was, like the old man said, a good song. The voice and the words were both haunting and mesmerizing.

When the song ended, we just stood there and held each other for a moment longer, gazing into one another's eyes. Then I turned to ask the man the name of the song.

He said, If and the singer's name, I believe, is Tom Marks."

Both Amy and I just stood there, frozen, then tearing.

"Did you say, Tom Marks?"

"Yeah, I believe that was his name. Why?"

Visibly sobbing now, I said, "That was my grandfather. I never heard his music before. He just died a few days ago, and we attended his funeral today."

"Sorry son, I didn't mean to stir up any bad memories."

"Oh no, this actually has been the perfect ending to the day, like it was his finale. For some reason, he loved this old place. I guess he had a lot of memories here and now he has created one for us. Thank you."

I turned to Amy and said, "Ready to go?"

"Yeah, but who's driving?"

"I told ya I had it under control. Trust me?"

"Do I have a choice? We're not sailing home are we?"

"No, not going home."

"What?"

"You heard me; it's not safe to drive home. I thought we'd get a room at the old Ramada where my Big Guy and Nan met."

"And you consider that safe?"

"Nope, romantic."

"Now who's being pushy?"

"Me."

"Well, this is a first. Mr. Banos, I guess I am under your spell. It does feel romantic. Just don't get us killed on the way, please. It would *ruing* my evening."

"Whatever m'lady desires."

"Oh, you are looking for trouble, aren't you?"

"Aye, and adventure."

"Sail on, Captain. Sail on."

AFTER WE CHECKED IN, we took the elevator up to our room where we were greeted by a balcony overlooking the ocean on the seventh floor.

"Oh, this is just lovely," Amy said as she laid on the bed. "And these mattresses are so comfortable."

"Oh, I bet," I said, as I laid beside her, kissing her deeply.

"Sonny, let's take this slow. I want this evening to last."

"Me too. Are you hungry?"

"As a matter of fact, I am, but do you think the dining room is still open. It's almost eleven."

"Well, we can go see."

And down we went to check it out.

"Hey, they don't close on the weekends until twelve. What luck?"

So, we went inside and were escorted to our table.

"Here is the dinner menu, sir. Would you like a cocktail?"

"That would be nice. What would you like Amy?"

"Chivas, neat please."

Astounded, I said, "Make that two, please."

As the waiter left, I said, "That threw me off guard. I didn't know you were a scotch drinker."

"Guess I had better be, hanging around with the Banos Boys," she said laughing.

I really had missed that laugh. I had been so involved in my career and looking after Big Guy that I never had much time left over for any social life. Now, I was sitting here, with this beautiful, blonde-haired little spitfire, who I used to think of more as a tomboy, looking deeply into her hazel blue eyes, which were showing me a whirlwind of emotions and anticipation.

Our waiter arrived with our drinks and asked, "Have you decided?"

"I think we will start with the shrimp cocktails and then have the tuna. Okay with you?"

"Perfect."

"How would you like your tuna prepared?

"Seared and rare?"

"I looked over at Amy, and she responded, "Absolutely, is there any other way?"

The waiter continued, "Stuffed baked potatoes or rice pilaf?"

Again glancing in Amy's direction, "Potatoes?"

"Sounds good. And blue cheese on the salads, if that's okay with you, Sonny."

"Fine by me."

"Excellent sir. I will have your shrimp cocktails right out," said the waiter as he turned and headed toward the kitchen.

As the waiter brought out the shrimp, Amy's hair shimmered in the candlelight as the two gazed out of the restaurant window looking at the ocean.

"I just had a deja vu moment, well, not really deja vu as it was somebody else's moment."

"What?" Amy giggled.

"Well, Big Guy was getting me to write down his memoirs, and there was this one story where he met Nan and took her to dinner here. THIS is pretty much the way that I had imagined it."

"Who knows what the future will hold. Maybe history will repeat itself."

"Well, I hope not completely. If all of Big Guy's stories were true, I am not sure I would want a repeat of that," I said laughing.

After we finished a delectable meal, we ventured out on the boardwalk heading for the beach. We walked down the beach in the dark, with the waves breaking against the shoreline.

"I wonder if this was how it was for your grandparents...walking down the beach, arm in arm underneath the moonbeams," said Amy dreamily.

"I have no doubt," I said, sighing.

Amy reached up and kissed me, and I returned the kiss. We then turned toward the ocean and gazed out at its splendor. I wondered what secrets the waves held as they clapped against the shore. I reached down and held Amy's hand tightly, our palms whispering our own secrets to one another as we walked back to the hotel. I, then, went into the lounge to retrieve a bottle of champagne.

"Uh-oh. Looks like I might be in trouble now."

"Maybe."

After we got inside our room, I uncorked the wine and poured two glasses. We lifted them and gave a final toast to our host.

"To you Big Guy, thanks for the memories."

"And for enabling some new ones," Amy said as she tackled me landing over on the bed.

We just started laughing uncontrollably. Then our eyes met as I caressed her skin and brushed back her hair. We locked love's embrace, as our lips met, never closing our eyes. I felt a passion that I had never felt before. It was exhilarating, as we enjoyed every subtle touch.

Then she paused and said, "There's something that I need to tell you. I have never...well, been with a man. I know I'm thirty, but, I have been so busy with everything, my education, my job, that...well, I have just never done it."

I start laughing, and she began to get mad. Then I said, "Wait! You don't understand. I'm not laughing at you. I just...well, I have never done it either. I have never been interested in anyone but you anyway. Like yourself, I have been busy cramming life into everything else around me, and I guess I never found the time, until now."

I looked at her with a lingering look, and she kissed me deeply and somehow, we managed. Oh, did we manage.

As the sun arose on our balcony, she grabbed my shirt to put on. She said, "It's going to be a long month."

"Yeah," sighing as I held her tightly, "a long month. Come on; we had better get dressed and head back."

"Before we do, could we take one last walk on *our beach*?"

"Surely."

"What? My name's not Shirley! It's Amy."

"You sounded just like Nan! Old family joke. I meant, of course, we can."

We walked along in the bright sunlight as Amy noticed something up ahead of us.

"Oh look," she said. "It's a starfish."

"Well, that is a good omen. Nan found one on the morning that she *bumped* into Big Guy. Toss it back into the ocean to give it new life, and maybe we will be blessed with a new life as well."

Together, they gently tossed the creature back into the sea.

"I guess we had better gather our stuff and get going. I still have a plane to catch."

"I wish you didn't have to leave today."

"The sooner I leave, the sooner I return."

"That's a plus."

"If you'd like, you could drive me to the airport."

"I think I would like that very much."

We went back upstairs and grabbed the few things we had brought and hurried back downstairs.

"Here," tossing Amy the keys, "go get the car, and I will check us out."

"And *I* will be checking *you* out Mr. Banos," said Amy, tossing her hair back as she exited the hotel.

"Banos? Did someone say, Banos? Are you related to Mark Banos?"

"Why yes, I'm Sonny Banos, Big Guy's...I mean Mark's grandson," I said directing my answer toward a red-haired older gentleman wearing a worn oxford shirt, khaki shorts, white socks, and sandals. I could tell he had spent his life at the beach by his well-weathered complexion, but his face didn't disclose his age...he was just old.

Turning toward the desk clerk the old man said, "Comp his bill in full. Mr. Banos' money is no good here."

"What? What do you mean? Why would you do that?"

"I'm Melvin, the hotel owner. Your grandfather and his band used to play here for the cover charge they took in at the door when we first opened. That really helped me out as I didn't have the budget for entertainment. Mark, or Tom Marks as he was known, used to bring in quite a crowd. That was one part of this hotel that I didn't have to worry about while he was here. Guess I should've told him that. Well, the bottom line is, we became lifelong friends, and I was glad to see him and his family move back to the area. I was sorry to hear about his passing.

Sorry, I couldn't make the funeral, but I had duties here that needed to be taken care of, so the least I can do is pay for his grandson's night at the inn. I hope you enjoyed your stay and will come to see me again."

"I did, and I will. It was nice to meet you, Mervin," I said with a mischievous grin.

"That's Melvin. Another typical Dumb Ass Banos Boy."

"It's a cross I have to bear," I said, placing the back of my hand on my forehead.

"See you later, son. I gotta make sure those umbrellas and chairs are put up. See you."

"See you, Melvin...and thanks."

My mouth was wide open as I walked out the door and got into the car.

Amy said, "Is everything alright?"

"Fine," I said in a daze as I revealed the conversation that I had had with Melvin at the front desk. It was one final tribute to the old man that I had loved so much.

Chapter Three

*A*my had to hurry so she could catch her flight back to Galveston, so we stopped by the Miller's to pick up her luggage and then barreled down highway 70 toward the Raleigh airport. Although it was over a two-hour drive, it was not nearly long enough to sort through all of the emotions we were discovering. It was now clear to me that I was desperately, head over heels in love with this woman, whom I had known for the biggest part of my teen and adult life. Funny how life takes you on journeys just to end up back where you started.

We arrived at RDU about an hour before her flight, which would give her just enough time to check her baggage, get frisked by the TSA and get on board.

Amy said, "Look, maybe this month will give us some time to sort out where we want to go from here. There's no rush. After all, we have been hanging around for the past 15 years. I don't think a month will kill us."

And with that, she gave me a hug and one of those long kisses that almost prompted me to buy a ticket, but I resisted the temptation.

"Slow and steady wins the race," I said grinning.

"I have no doubt," she said blowing me a kiss.

As she ran down the runway entrance, she looked back one more time and smiled. I smiled as well. As a matter of fact, I couldn't get my mouth off of my ears for the next two hours on the ride back to New Bern. She promised she'd call when she landed, and of course, I kept my phone next to me looking at the time every few minutes.

As I pulled into the driveway, my phone rang. It was Amy.

"Long time no see."

"I know," she said. "I just touched down. Where are you?"

"Just pulling into the driveway."

"Good, you're safe then."

"I'm glad you are too."

"Well, I gotta go get my luggage. I will call you later once I get home and pour me some scotch."

"Now you're beginning to sound like a Banos. Hey, you mean I gotta wait to hear from you again until you get back home to New Bern?"

"No silly, I mean when I get to my apartment. Talk to you then."

"Oh. okay, Amy, I..." but the phone went dead.

Feeling slightly embarrassed, I headed towards the empty house before me. Mom and Dad said they were going to get out today and maybe run down to Beaufort to clear their heads before returning to Toronto. I went inside, poured myself a scotch, and sat down and listened to some soft music on Pandora, John Tesh radio I think it was, as I drifted off into my thoughts. All I could think about was the night before, and Amy, seeing her over and over again in my mind. Her image was so crystal clear that I couldn't help but think she was right in front of me.

A few hours later, Mom and Dad arrived back at the house and announced that they were heading back tomorrow.

"Yeah, we thought we might as well get on back. Are you going to be okay now?"

"Sure Dad. I have been here by myself for some time. I just

don't have Big Guy to visit every day now. That's really all that's changed."

"Well, it might be a good idea to sort through your grandparents' belongings, and anything that you don't want to hang onto you can give to Goodwill. We don't need anything to take back to Canada with us, so feel free to dispose of the stuff in any way that you see fit."

"That could turn out to be a hard job."

"No rush, just leave it until you are ready. I just wanted to let you know you could get rid of it, in case it gets in your way."

"So, how's it going with you and Amy?" Angel asked slyly.

"Mom, we may be heading into some uncharted waters."

Laughing Mom said, "Well, it wouldn't be the first time. Take it slow. It will happen when the time is right."

"I know. It just seems like we have wasted a lot of time already."

"You both just needed time to grow. We'll see what the future holds. A death in the family sometimes allows us to re-evaluate our priorities."

"Yeah, it sure does seem that way," I said.

"Hey, you guys hungry?" asked Vinnie.

"You betcha," we said.

"How 'bout some Carolina Barbecue?"

"With hot slaw?" we teased.

"You betcha!"

So we piled into the car and left for the Big Oaks Drive-In singing,

BODI, BODI, BODI, BODI, BO!

AMY CALLED AGAIN LATER that night, once we got back from eating.

"Hi ya," said Amy.

"Hi ya back," I said.

"What 'cha been doing?"

"Just eating and drinking with the fam. They are leaving to go back to Canada tomorrow."

"Are you going to be okay by yourself?"

"Sure, I've been that way for the past few years now. Of course, it would be nice if I had a friend a little closer by."

"Yeah," she said sighing, "I know what you mean. I really miss you already."

"Yeah, me too."

"So what are your plans for this evening."

"Pizza and pack up."

"Sounds like a plan. Wish I was there to help you."

"I wish you were, too."

"You know Amy, there is something I have been meaning to tell you."

"And what might that be?" she said giggling.

"Well, I think I'm falling..."

Just then Amy's doorbell rang, and she said, "I've got to answer that. I'll call you right back."

"Okay, bye."

But she didn't. That was the longest night I can ever remember. What was going on? Who was at the door? Did she just forget to call me back? My sleepless night finally ended with me stumbling into the kitchen to fix myself breakfast, which consisted of leftover barbecue and a Blue Moon. Mom and Dad got up a couple of hours later, packed up and headed out the door.

"You gonna be alright?" Mom said.

"Sure thing. You guys drive safe and call me when you reach Toronto."

"We will, son," said Vinnie. "We'll see you again soon."

After exchanging hugs, I watched as they headed down the road, Standing there, I began to realize that there had been so much hustle and bustle during the last few days, it now seemed as if the world had come to a screeching halt. I could hear the clock in the living room ticking. Eerie silence.

About half-past ten, the doorbell rang. Now, who in the world could that be? I really didn't feel like company.

"Surprise, it's me!"

Dazed and confused, I just stood there unable to utter a sound. Tears of joy sprang from my eyes as I plainly beheld a vision, no a daydream, of the woman I loved and so desperately needed at that very moment.

"Are you not going to invite me in?" the vision said.

Wiping my eyes, I reached out to hug her and swing her around in my arms. Our eyes met, and then we kissed, one of THOSE kisses.

"God, I am so glad to see you! But how? Why are you here and not in Galveston?"

"Long story. I answered the door after I hung up with you, and it was my boss. He came by to tell me that everyone had packed my stuff up at work and that he was going to send the movers over to pack up and take care of everything in my apartment. He, then, gave me a severance check and wished me well, after thanking me for all of the work I had done for him. He told me goodbye and that he would miss me and then handed me a plane ticket, so here I am...for good!"

"Mann, this is great! Wow, this is the best surprise I could have ever imagined."

"Now, I have one question for you? What were you going to tell me before my doorbell rang?" she asked, eyes dancing.

"I was going to say," stammering while I revealed the secret that was in my heart, "well...I'm afraid that I am hopelessly in love with you and ask you what you're doing for the rest of your life. Will you be my wife?"

"Oh, Sonny. I love you too, I always have and yes, of course, I will."

Chapter Four

A June wedding on the beach is always beautiful. Everyone dresses in white, and the sun is always shining. We reserved a spot near the front of the old Ramada. Fitting, we thought, as we kinda already had the honeymoon there, plus it's been the family landmark for decades.

We decided not to have much pomp and circumstance since there were just us, the Millers and my parents. Uncle Marty had declined the invitation since his health was failing. He was afraid the walk down the beach in the heat would be too much for him. Amy invited Leah, a former classmate, to be her maid of honor and I, of course, chose my dad as best man. Mr. Miller walked his daughter down the dunes to the ocean, where we began the ceremony. I have never seen Amy so beautiful. She was positively glowing, with the breeze gently blowing her white dress, as she walked, barefooted in the sand. And I have never been so nervous in all of my life, fidgeting and sweating profusely. Then came the vows.

"Do you Sonny, take Amy to be your lawfully wedded wife, to have and to hold, for better or worse, for richer or poorer for as long as you both shall live?"

"Yep, I do," I said, thinking that I just sounded like the Jeff Dunham puppet named Peanut.

Amy giggled and then turned toward me as the preacher said, "And do you Amy take Sonny to be your lawfully wedded husband, to have and to hold, for better or worse, for richer or poorer for as long as you both shall live?"

"As long as he promises not to take me sailing, of course, I do!"

Everyone burst into laughter, and the preacher said, "By the powers vested in me by the state of North Carolina, I now pronounce you husband and wife. You may kiss your bride."

We kissed, and everyone cheered and clapped and the preacher yelled, "Mazeltov!" as he quickly stomped on an inverted dixie cup causing it to make a loud *"POP"!*

Everyone stopped and gasped in amazement.

He just said, "I have always wanted to shout that at a wedding, and I just couldn't imagine saying it at a more appropriate wedding than yours. It means *Good Luck*. You kids are gonna need it. Oy Vey," he said as he turned to walk down the beach toward the Ramada.

Everyone shrugged and laughed as we started posing for pictures. Then, everyone headed to the hotel where an intimate reception for the families was waiting. There were heavy hors d'oeuvres and of course, scotch as well as Blue Moons and Miller High Life, in honors of Amy's family, for the occasion.

Getting to know Billy and Elva better was a real pleasure these past few months before the wedding. They were in their late fifties, a little older than Mom and Dad, but with about the same amount of grey and laugh lines. Billy was slightly balding with a pouch... not fat mind you, but an obvious love for eating. Elva was about the same shape and frame as Mom, although you could tell, she did a good bit more manual labor than Mom. We started to grow rather close, spending almost every Sunday eating dinner with them. Funny, we had known each other since I was 15, but Amy and I just never hung around her parents much. Shame, they were delightful people with lots of stories of their own.

I loved the one about Amy trying to find out if Santa was real. It seems that the only one she would share her Christmas list with was the department store Santa. Billy and Elva, try as they might, could not get Amy to share any of her Christmas wishes with them. Come Christmas, there were lots of toys under the tree, but not the ones that Amy had asked from Santa. Billy ran out to the store the next day and bought every toy that she had asked for, but it just wasn't the same magic as before. She had *ruinged* Christmas, as she said. It became a perennial favorite.

Looking at my beloved, I said, "Sorry if my nerves *ruinged* the ceremony."

"It was perfect, and I will go sailing with you anytime, Captain," she said as she winked.

"You know as much as I hate it, we had better wrap this up if we are going to get to Charleston tonight."

"Good idea. CATCH!" Amy yelled as she threw the bouquet to Leah. "I gots me some bones to jump," causing me to blush. Everyone else just laughed. Typical Carteret County Amy.

OUR DRIVE to Charleston was a rather long one, but the five and a half hours flew by as we talked the whole way, thinking only about our destination. We arrived at the Planters Inn around 10 pm, but wide awake with excitement and anticipation of our new life together. After checking in, the porter carried our luggage to our suite. Following him, we approached the doorway, and the porter opened the door. I swooped Amy into my arms and carried her across the threshold.

"Whew! You really know how to sweep a girl off her feet."

"Oh, I think I will even get better at it with a little practice," I said.

Tipping the porter and bidding him goodnight, we were finally on our own; our first real night together.

"Will you look at this?" said Amy pointing to the table at the window. "What a beautiful arrangement of flowers. And the room is beautiful. Would you come and look at this spectacular view?"

"And look," I said, "there is a bucket of champagne and a plate of chocolate covered strawberries. Yum!"

I popped the cork and poured our first toast. "To a long and happy life together."

"With my forever love," echoed Amy.

Munching down on the strawberries, we suddenly realized that we had not eaten anything since the reception.

"I'm about to starve," said Amy.

"I guess we had better find out quickly what this town has in the way of restaurants open at this hour," I said.

Before I could barely get those words out of my mouth, there was a knock at the door.

"Yes?"

"Room service."

"Room service?" I said puzzled. "But we didn't order anything."

"It was ordered for you."

Opening the door, a man proceeded to wheel in a cart and set up our table by the window.

He then revealed a succulent dinner of poached red snapper in papaya and mango sauce, accompanied with rice pilaf, and parmesan encrusted asparagus. After the table was set and the meal placed he asked, "Will there be anything else?"

We both just stood there like store mannequins as the waiter prepared to leave.

"Who did all of this?" Amy finally blurted out.

"Oh, I was to give you this card. I almost forgot. Mr. Vincent Banos sent it to the hotel concierge to give you. Have a good evening."

Amy opened the card, turned white and handed it to me.

"What's wrong?" I said.

"Read the card."

As I read, tears filled my eyes. I recognized the handwriting immediately.

"We *wanted you to have a beautiful honeymoon just like we did. A wonderful man provided everything our hearts could desire on ours, and we wanted to make sure your first evening together was as special as ours. Enjoy the roses, strawberries, champagne, and dinner on us. May you and Amy have a wonderful life. Remember, NO SAILING! We Banos' aren't very good at it. Until we meet again. Love you both, Big Guy and Nan.*"

"How did they know? How did they know you would marry me?" asked Amy.

Catching my breath, I managed to utter, "How could they not know?"

WE DID SET sail the next day for the Bahamas, although I was not at the helm.

It was a fun Carnival Cruise, where we spent the next several days and nights emerged in the experience of our first cruise. We sampled every culinary treat, watched every show and danced until we couldn't dance anymore. The nights, after dancing, were incredibly intense, as well as the morning and then there were the nooners. I had married a sex-a-holic. YES! But all too quickly, we settled back into the routine of work and responsibilities.

The nights were still there, at least three, but the morning opening exercises quickly faded, as did the nooners. Then, one morning, "Oh my God!" Amy yelled as she ran to the bathroom puking.

A minute later I was right behind her tossing cookies. Then it stopped as quickly as it came upon us.

I said, "What the hell did we eat last night? I haven't thrown up like that in years."

"A broccoli stuffed baked potato and a salad. Nothing that would have done this I wouldn't think."

We started to feel better and dismissed it to allergies or sinuses. Then we got dressed and ready to go to work. Thank God it was

Friday, so if we did end up getting sick, we wouldn't have to be somewhere tomorrow.

And tomorrow came, and I awoke to, "Oh no..." as Amy hit the head again. And a few minutes later I was right beside her.

"Shit! What is going on with us?"

"I don't know, but I am feeling really weird, and I haven't had a period in two months."

"You don't suppose...?"

"Oh God, one of those little Banos swimmers breached the dam!"

We both sat down on the edge of the bed and said, "Oh God."

"What do we do now?" I said.

"Well, I guess we have to find out if the rabbit dies."

"What?" I said looking over at Amy in puzzlement.

"That's an old expression because doctors used to inject a rabbit's ovaries with the patient's urine sample to examine under a microscope to see if she was pregnant."

"What happened to the rabbit after removing her ovaries? Did they put them back?"

"No, the rabbit died."

"That's pretty barbaric. Why didn't they just use one of those test kits?"

"They didn't always have those."

"Oh," I moaned, "Well, I guess we better go find a rabbit then."

"Yeah, right after breakfast. I'm starving."

"Oh shit. You probably are pregnant. But why am I throwing up? I'm not pregnant."

"*We're* pregnant. You are having sympathy pains."

"Oh Christ, I can't wait for labor. Yippee."

After breakfast, we went to the pharmacy to get one of THOSE kits. I felt like I was in there buying my first pack of rubbers. I was beginning to think that maybe I should have bought more. How am I going to raise a kid? Am I even father material? Then I got to thinking. Dad raised me. Did he have the same thoughts and apprehensions? I didn't come with an owner's manual. Well, how tough could it be? I'd just teach him to fish and ride a bike and play baseball and sail...well, maybe not sail. Oh shit, what if it's a girl? What the fuck do I do then?

"What 'cha thinkin' about Daddy?"

"Huh...what? Oh, nothing. Let's get home so we can find out if *we're* pregnant or just coming down with the flu."

"Maybe the old poo flu," she said sighing.

"Hey, I didn't mean anything by it. I am just anxious to see what's going on and then we can go from there."

"Where are you planning to go?"

"I'm not going anywhere, not now, not ever. Give me a break. You're turning my words around. Let's just go home."

"Are you sure you want to?"

"YES!"

"Why are you yelling at me?"

"I didn't mean to yell. I just want to know is all."

"Well, if you really want to."

"I REALLY WANT TO."

"Okay! FINE."

Once home, she took the kit into the bathroom. Struggling with the package, she almost dropped the stick in the toilet.

"Quick and easy my ass," she said exasperatedly.

After taking the test, she waited for the results...and waited...and waited, then...

"Oh my God! We're pregnant! We are going to be parents!"

Running in the bathroom, I picked Amy up and swung her around in the air.

"We're going to be parents!" I said, as our lips met. Then everything stopped...all sound and movement stopped...the world and everything in it stopped...as we whispered and it finally sunk in,

"We're going to be parents..."

Chapter Five

"*H*ello, Mom? It's me."

"Sonny? Are you and Amy alright. You usually don't call us until Sunday. What's up, eh?"

"Mom, put us on FaceTime so we can all see each other."

"Okay, I'll call your father. VINNIE, COME DOWN TO THE PHONE, IT'S SONNY."

"You got it now?"

"Yeah, here we go. I can see you all now. So, what's cooking?"

"Well, it's more like what's been baked. The buns in the oven!"

"Are guys shitting me? You're going to have a baby?"

"Yes, we are. We're pregnant!"

"How did that happen?" said Vinnie, "I meant how did WE become pregnant...I mean you? Jeez."

"We say WE because we both came down with morning sickness."

"Oh, that. So, did your dad, although he doesn't like to recall it."

"I *recalled* enough then, thank you."

"Okay, Vinnie, enough. This is exciting! I am so happy for you two. We'll plan a couple of trips down, once you get farther along.

One for a baby shower and a second one to help you when the baby first comes home. Sopie and Mark stayed with us a couple of weeks when you were first born, and it really helped us out."

"Yeah, it was an eye-opener for Mark," Vinnie said laughing. "You pissed in his eye and crapped all over the house because he put the diaper on backward."

"I didn't hear about that one before!"

"He swore me to secrecy and told me he'd have me killed if I ever told anyone," Vinnie said laughing.

"When did you find out, Amy?"

"Just this morning."

"Well, make sure you find a good doctor, Honey. You need good prenatal care for you and the baby."

"Oh, I will call first thing Monday. This is just starting to sink in. I know now why you have to wait nine months. It will take that long just to get everything ready."

"Yes, there will be lots to do."

I said,"Well Mom, Dad, we need to get off the phone, so we can go tell Billy and Elva."

"Okay, we love you. Tell them *Hi* for us."

"We'll tell them. We love you both, too. Goodbye."

We then picked ourselves up and drove to the Millers.

"Well, this is a surprise!" said Elva. "You two are usually gala-vanting around the island on Saturday. To what do we two old codgers owe this pleasure?"

"We have exciting news!"

"Oh God, you didn't let him buy a sailboat did you?" said Billy.

"No, to the hell no, never. We're pregnant!"

"Oh, there for a minute I thought...What did you say?"

"We're pregnant! You're gonna be grandparents!"

"Wowee! I'm gonna be a Pop-Pop! And you're gonna be a Mom-mom."

"I think he took the news rather well," said Elva. "Congratulations you two. I am so excited for all of us. Have you told Vinnie and Angel yet, Sonny?"

"Yes, we just got off the phone with them before we came over and oh, they said to say hello. They were so shocked but excited."

"Well, we are shocked too, but the one thing I will not have to worry about is how good the two of you will be at becoming great parents."

"That's for sure. This calls for a celebration. Scotch, Sonny?"

"Oh, yeah. I am beginning to need a drink."

"Me too," said Amy.

"Sorry honey," said Elva, "Your next drink will come in about seven months."

"Now that sucks," said Amy, "but I suppose it a small sacrifice to make sure this baby is as healthy as he can be."

"Come on outside. We'll chat some more, and a little later I'll fire up the grill and put on some rib-eyes for dinner," said Billy.

"Sounds great!" said everyone and they proceeded to the back-yard patio.

Savoring the scotch, Billy turned to Amy and asked, "Y'all thought of any names for the baby yet?"

"We haven't even had time for this to sink in yet, let alone discuss names."

"We'll just don't come up with some weird long Greek name like Achilles or Adonis or Thomas Sopoulos," Billy said grinning, looking over at Sonny.

"Maybe we'll do like my mom and dad did and have one of those long formal Greek names that nobody can pronounce, but nickname him Fido, or something like that," I countered.

"Him? What makes you think it's going to be a boy?" chimed in Amy.

"Cause we Banos' always have boys."

"Oh, you're right. It couldn't possibly be a girl. That's why they call them Dabbs," said Amy.

"I don't understand, honey," said Elva. "What's a Dabb?"

"Dumb Ass Banos Boy."

"Oh, dear," said Elva quietly withdrawing from the conversation. She then began, "Do you think it's going to snow tomorrow?"

Amy and I soon got busy with planning the baby's room.

"I think the crib would look nice over here with one of those cute hanging mobiles above it. The changer could go here and the bureau over there. I want this room to be soothing but colorful. What do you think?"

"I think it sounds wonderful. I am totally at your disposal."

"Well, speaking of disposal, don't you think it's time to go through your grandparent's things and dispose of what you don't want to keep."

"Yeah, I suppose it is past time with the baby coming and all. I guess I'll get started on it next weekend."

Saturday came, and I, true to my word, began the daunting task of sorting through all of my grandparent's old belongings.

"I never realized they were such pack rats," I said.

"It looks like this may take you a while. Do you want some help?"

"No, not right now. I've got to go through this stuff and make sure I don't toss anything of real value."

"Okay, but I'm here if you need me."

"Thanks, Honey."

I spent most of the day going through the clothes and checking pockets, as the old man was known for leaving a few dollars in them. I found about $633 before I lost count. Jeez!

Then, after gathering the clothes, I started the formidable task of going through the memorabilia. I came across the manuscript that Big Guy and I had begun to work on. It was intact, and I remembered my promise to get his story out. So I decided that I would tackle that project as soon as the baby was born. Then I came upon Nan's hope chest. It didn't have much in it other than an old coat and parka, some love letters that Big Guy had sent her, an old porcelain doll with a cracked face and what is this?...a diary?

I started to open it and then hesitated...this was private. Maybe

I didn't have a right to look into her private thoughts. I shut the trunk and went about my tasks of cleaning up. But the book kept calling me...luring me to peek into her past.

So I stopped, sat down and opened the book. As I started to read, I realized that these entries filled in the gaps in Big Guy's stories. Were they really true?

June 29th, 1975. I was at the beach with my parents. This morning I met a wonderful man named Tom. He invited me to dinner. Now, all I have to do is decide whether to wear the yellow or the blue dress.

I went to have dinner with Tom. When I got to the lobby, I got a real surprise. It turns out that Tom Marks is the entertainer in the nightclub, a little detail he left out. We had dinner, and then we walked on the beach, and then he invited me to come to his show, which I did, but I had to be careful not to stay too late as the parents would be mad. He electrified the crowd. It was amazing. Then he dimmed the lights and dedicated a song, "If" to me, Sopie, which is what he calls me. I don't mind; I think it's sweet. Then he ends the song by handing me a rose and kisses me. The crowd goes wild. I was kinda embarrassed, but at the same time exhilarated.

Oh my God, I thought, this was the same song that Amy and I danced to at the Beach Tavern. I continued to read.

Mama and Papa were so mad at me when I arrived late in the room. They said we are leaving tomorrow. Will I ever see Tom again?

June 30th, 1975. I went out to the beach to see Tom one last time and gave him my picture and phone number. He took me upstairs to his room and gave me an old necklace that his grandmother gave him. I will never take it off.

July 5, 1975. Tom calls me every day. We don't really talk about much, yet we talk about everything. He is so special. Today, he sent me roses. I just cried and cried when I got them.

Then, he called later, and somehow he tricked me into saying I loved him. He was right. I do love him. Then he asked me to marry him. Before I could even think I blurted out, yes, of course, I will.

Then I felt foolish but extremely happy. He said he would come and see me in a couple of weeks. I can't wait.

July 20th, 1975. Tom came to my house and we were so happy. He was nervous when Mama and Papa arrived home from church. The tension was so thick. I just think Papa was being protective of me. We had dinner, a very quiet dinner and then I suggested we meet some friends in town so that I could rescue my love. We went to a local club where we met up with Joey and Roxanne. Joey plays guitar, and he and Tom hit it off right away. We had such a fantastic time dancing. Oh, how I wish it never had to end. I asked Joey to show Tom around town the next day while I went to work.

July 21st, 1975. After leaving Tom asleep on the couch, I went to work in a daydream, thinking about Tom and maybe he'd stop by. Then I got word that Mr. Figerino wanted to see me.

Oh boy, I thought, maybe he was going to give me a promotion. I was totally shocked by what I saw in his office. There was Mr. Figerino, Papa, and William. They told me that they had decided that I would send Tom packing and marry William or William was to kill him. Devastated, I went home with William who stood behind me at the door with a gun as Tom arrived. I told Tom it was over, that I had decided that marrying him was just not a good idea. Tom took off, mad at the world. I cried all night but knew it was the only way to keep Tom alive.

"Oh my God," I cried out.

"What is it, Honey."

"You are never going to believe what I found."

"What?"

"Nan's diary and it is unbelievable. It tells her whole story about how she and Big Guy met and why they didn't get together for so long. I just can't put it down."

"Let me see."

"Wow! It says she was forced to marry this gangster creep, William, who treated her like shit and oh my God, he raped her."

"What?"

"Yeah, she says he raped her one night when he was drunk playing cards...to teach her a lesson."

"That's just sickening. Let me see that again. Now, this is strange...she also says that while he was beating her, an eerie green light flooded the room and just as William was about to punch her, he was propelled into the wall. Then, he tried to hit her again, and again he flew back into the wall. Dazed, he left the room, and she saw Tom's face disappear with the green light."

"God, that gives me chills. I wonder what that was all about?" said Amy.

"I have no idea, but Big Guy told me some weird tales in his memoirs that kinda match up with Nan's diary. I thought it was just the embellished ramblings of an old man. Do you suppose it could all be true?"

"Maybe, Nan was pretty young when she wrote these entries in her diary. And most people spill their heart out in a diary. They are not likely to embellish."

"I'm starting to get a little hungry. You want to order a pizza?"

"Yeah, with pickles."

"Okay, enough."

Once dinner arrived, we sat down on the floor eating pizza and continued to read, mesmerized by every entry.

August 13th, 1978. This morning Mama came over. She noticed right away that I had been beaten and said I needed to go home with her, but William came home and stopped me.

Mama called me later that night and told me to pack a suitcase as we were leaving for good.

August 14th, 1978. Papa and Mama didn't show up. William did. He told me that they had been killed in a car crash. Oh God, what will I do? I am all alone now.

August 17th, 1978. My parent's funeral. A very sad day. I overheard William and Sal talking. Something about accidents do happen. I now wonder if William had something to do with my parents' death.

"This just gets worse and worse," I said, "How could she stay with that monster?"

"I'm not sure she had any choice. You saw what they said about killing Tom."

"Yeah, I know. It's hard to believe my Nan could live through this ordeal and what she must have had to endure."

Picking up the leftover pizza out of the floor and heading to the kitchen, Amy said, "It's getting late. Are you ready for bed."

"Yeah, but if it's okay, I'm going to take this with me and read a little more."

October 18, 1979. Living alone all day with no one to talk to, I started having conversations with my old porcelain doll Mama and Papa had given me. "Effie" had always been my confidant and it was no surprise how she provided me with some comfort during these horrible days. Today, William caught me talking to Effie, and he threw her up against the wall breaking her face. I was so mad that, although I don't remember hitting William, he flew against the wall knocking him unconscious. I went ahead and fixed dinner, and William finally came out dazed and sat down to eat in silence. I said something about accidents sometimes happen and he looked at his food and left out the door. I guess he thought I was going to poison him.

It was well past midnight when I finished reading the entries about her living with William and his gangland activities in Youngstown. I got to the part where he was supposed to carry out a hit on the county prosecutor for the mob. Nan had overheard the mobsters' plan and went to the FBI, where she met F.P. (I do wonder what that stood for) and she went into the witness protection program and moved to Chicago. Then I dozed off, book in hand.

Chapter Six

"*D*id you ever go to sleep or did you stay up all night reading?"

"I finally nodded off. Did you know that Nan was in the witness protection program?"

"No! Really! Was it because of that creep husband of hers?"

"Yeah, he was gonna kill the county prosecutor, and she overheard his plans."

"Wow!"

"Yeah, and then she went and met with Agent Kroner. You remember F.P.? Well, evidently he's the one that helped her and moved her to Chicago."

"I thought I heard she was in New Orleans when Big Guy met her."

"I don't know how all of that tied together. I evidently haven't got that far into her story yet."

"I haven't read about your grandfather's life yet, but if it is half as exciting as Nan's you ought to get someone to put it in novel form and publish it."

"Well, I promised Big Guy to do just that, so maybe after the baby's born. We'll see."

"I will see you this evening. I have got to get to work," he said leaning over to kiss Amy on the forehead.

"Yeah, me too. See ya tonight. I love you."

"Love you too."

"WHAT'S FOR DINNER? I could eat a whole cow," I said laughing as I came through the door.

"Would you settle for a itsy-bitsy cow? We're having hamburgers on the grill, Grillmeister."

"Okay by me. I'll go out and get it started. Have we got any of that new Caribbean beer left that I picked up the other day?"

"Yes, El Presidente, I believe there is one or two left in the fridge. Do you want fries and a salad to go along with the burgers?"

"Yeah, that sounds great. Let me get out there and do what a MAN does."

"Remember Sonny, that's flame kist, not flame crisp."

"Haha, very funny. I'll be back in a few."

Coming back in for another beer, I said, "Are those deviled eggs?"

"Yes, they are."

"I am one lucky man," I said giving her a love pat on the derrière.

"Yes, you are," Amy said punching me gently in the stomach. "Now get the hell out of here, hornball, and grill me some burgers."

"Check, Chief," I said running out the door.

That evening, right after dinner, I headed back to read more of the diary.

July 4th, 1990. I am finally free. It's a perfect day. The mob is in jail. I have finished testifying, and now I am here in Carol Stream, Illinois living in my apartment, alone. But free.

I found a job recently at a local Catholic Parrish, and I work with chil-

dren there. The nuns treat me so well, especially Amyra, who has taken me under her wing. She has helped me get in touch with my psychic abilities. I knew they were there, but she has shown me how to use them for the benefit of others.

Then I ran across an entry that was particularly interesting to me.

March 11th, 1991. The boy Vincent, that was dropped off at the church as an infant, comes to stay with me for good today. I have, as of today, legally adopted him. I hope I can be a good mother to him and he will grow up happy. I swear I will protect and love him with my whole heart, so help me God.

How about that! Dad was adopted. I never knew that. I wonder why he never told me.

"Are you still reading that diary?"

"Yeah, I just found out that Dad was adopted."

"No kidding."

"Mann, you talk about some family history."

"Well, we have some family history in the making, so how about getting busy and gather up the rest of the stuff you plan on giving to Goodwill."

"Okay, I guess I have gotten a little sidetracked lately."

The next day, I called Dad to tell him what I had found.

"Hi Mom, is Dad there?"

"He's laying down. He hasn't been feeling well lately."

"Oh, I'm sorry."

"Can I help you?"

"Well, I just wanted to tell him what I found sorting through Nan and Big Guy's stuff."

"What'd you find?"

"Nan's diary."

"What? I didn't know she even kept a diary."

"You wouldn't believe what family history I am finding, some good, some not so good. Did you know Dad was adopted?"

"Yes, Honey."

"Why didn't I know?"

"I guess it just never came up. Look, Son, I'd love to talk to you more about this, but right now I have to make some supper for your father. I'll talk to you later and tell your dad that you called."

"Okay, Mom. Tell him I hope he gets to feeling better soon."

"I will. Goodbye."

"Bye Mom."

THE NEXT FEW months passed quickly and were filled with getting the baby's room together, doctor visits and Lamaze classes. Mom and Dad were coming down next weekend to help with the baby shower. It would be good to see them again.

"Hi, Guys!" I said.

"Hi Honey, where's Amy?"

"She's resting. A couple of months left to go don't 'cha know?"

"Oh, I remember. Why do you think you are an only child?" said Mom laughing.

"Dad, come on in and take a load off, I'll tell Amy y'all are here."

Dad looked a little grayer and wearier than usual. I guess long drives are no longer his friend. He might consider flying. God knows he can afford it and it sure would be a lot less stressful for them both.

Amy stuck her head in the door and said, "Hello everybody, I'll be with y'all in a minute."

A few minutes later she reappeared. "Now, I am a little more presentable. This pregnancy thing is not what it's cracked up to be. My back hurts all the time. Well, enough about me, how are you guys doing? Long trip, eh?"

"It was a little more tiring than usual. We will probably retire early tonight to get a good night's rest so I can be fresh for the shower tomorrow. What are you boy's planning?" said Mom.

"You mean we don't have to go to the hen party, I mean, shower?" I said.

"Well, if you really want to..." said Amy slyly.

"No, I'm sure Dad has some great baby care advice he'd like to share with me, man to man, right Dad."

"Absolutely Sonny. I'm sure I have lots to share."

"The only thing you have to share is maybe some of that new scotch you came across," said Mom.

"Well, it's not the only thing."

"New scotch sounds interesting," I said.

"Well, it will have to wait until tomorrow. I am about to starve. You know anywhere we can get some Carolina Barbecue?"

"And hot slaw?"

"Yes, and hot slaw."

"I can maybe think of a place that might have some," I said wryly.

"Wait, I want a Shrimp Burger," said Mom.

"Gee, I don't think I know of a place that has both except maybe..."

And everyone shouted, "Big Oak Drive-In!"

"And Barbecue!" I added. "BODI, BODI, BODI, BODI, BO!"

THE NEXT DAY THE HENS, (oops! ladies) headed for Elva's while Dad and I beamed (pun intended) at the prospect of trying yet another, I'm sure, marvelous scotch. When the ladies were out of sight, I said, "Well Pops, what'cha got?"

"Something you are likely never to see again. I happened upon an obscure little liquor store in Pittsburg on the way down. It seems he bought this bottle of Japanese Whiskey that he thought would be a good seller, but as luck would have it, most of his patrons were Irish and hardcore Jameson fanatics. So, this has been sitting on the shelf for the last 35 years," he said as he revealed the contents of the bag.

"Oh my God! It's a bottle of a 2013 Sherry Cask Yamazaki 18-

year-old. The best whiskey in the world! It doesn't even exist. You must have paid a fortune for that."

"Not really. The shop owner practically begged me to take it off his hands. I think he sold it to me, pretty much at cost. I think it was around $1800."

"Jesus! That stuff sold for $3000 when it was first bottled. Good deal, Dad. Can we try it?"

"Collecting is for pussies. Yes, we can try it."

That first taste was an experience that I remember to this day. An incredible aroma filled the air as soon as the alcohol evaporated. It was truly Nirvana.

"When I get to Heaven, I am going to order a case," said Dad.

"Do you think they have scotch in Heaven?"

"If they don't, I going to Hell. I'm sure that's where Big Guy will be."

"Good thing we don't use ice."

"Yes, son. it's a good thing we don't use ice."

"Dad, speaking of Big Guy, did Mom tell you that I ran across Nan's diary?"

"Yes, she did."

"I never realized you were adopted. Why didn't you ever tell me?"

"It just never came up. I guess now since you are getting ready to have a son of your own, it might be a good time to shed some light on some things that you will never know unless I tell you."

Dad poured some more scotch and offered me some. Then he said, "Let's go sit outside, it's a nice day. This story may take a while."

With that, we proceeded to the back deck that overlooked the Neuse River. It was one of those beautiful sunny days with no breeze at all, and the water was shimmering with sailboats floating out into the channel giving the appearance of those boats that you buy in gift shops sitting on mirrors. Dad just reared back in his rocker, sipped on his scotch and began to tell his tale.

"Sonny, as you know, I have been heavily involved in creating

Wifi television throughout Canada. You also know, that I started with a deep-rooted background in pure mathematics, which included subjects that weren't taught in college at the time, such as differential calculus, quantum physics, and string theory."

"Yeah, Dad, I took those courses as well, but I am not sure that I am onboard with all of those theories."

"We'll get back to that. Anyway, when I came up with the idea about Wifi television, I told F.P. that it was similar to Tesla's wireless electricity. At the time, however, I didn't realize how similar it was."

"What do you mean, Dad?"

"A few years ago, I decided to try and discover my birth heritage. So, I went to the Parrish in Carol Stream to see what I could find out. All I could find were the adoption records that were copies of those that Mom had. It listed a mother, Joan Tester and a father, Nicholas Tester.

I researched and googled but came up empty-handed. The only thing I found was an Elizabeth Joan Tester that died on October 23rd, 1991. There was no other information available and no mention of a Nicholas Tester or any husband or child for that matter."

"That's odd, go on."

"I was just about to go home when something told me to stop by the Parrish one more time. So I did and was greeted by a friendly nun that said she remembered my mom. I think she said her name was Amyra. Well, anyway, she said that my father brought me to the church. He was perplexed as to what to do with me. His wife had died three days after giving birth to me, and he could not stay here. He had to get back to where he was from, and he could not take me with him. When the sisters asked where he was from, he gave a year, 1928, not a place. His name was not Nicholas Tester, but Nikola Tesla!"

"Now you're shitting me right, eh? Good scotch story, Dad," I said rearing back laughing.

But Dad wasn't laughing. His look was stone cold. "Sonny,

there are a lot of things that we do not fully understand, even with our advanced mathematical backgrounds. Hell, we would have been ridden out of town on a rail back in the day. But, if you look closely at Tesla, the man, there were a lot of things that he invented that weren't even patented. He just wanted to get the ideas down, and I'm guessing, from what he had seen in the future."

"You know Dad, string theory gives the hypothesis for this possibility of traveling forward in time, and even returning using something they call tachyons, but no one has figured out how to do it yet."

"Well yes, someone had."

"Who, Tesla?"

"Yes, and your grandparents."

"Nan and Big Guy?"

"The same."

"Now I know this is some good scotch."

"It's not the scotch; it's the truth. And I thought you should hear it from me as you and I both at least have somewhat of a grasp on the scientific and not the science fiction."

"This sounds more like science fiction, like Big Guy's memoirs."

"As I told you before, I wouldn't discount that memoir as the ramblings of an old man. I think as you read through Mom's diary and listen to what I have to tell you, that you will be convinced that you come from a rather bizarre bunch."

"I always knew that," I said, again laughing.

"Well, this Sister Amyra filled me in on a lot about Mom that I sorta knew, but just shrugged it off, like the time she reasoned with a bear and later that same bear saved Mark's life."

"What?"

"Yeah, I was around sixteen or seventeen and had left the garbage bag outside the can, and a bear came to eat the trash. Mom shot at the bear and missed. The next thing I know is she goes in the house and gets a fish and tosses it to the bear. I asked her what just happened and she said she and the bear had come to an understanding. Weird! Now, the very next morning we are all out fishing and Mark's rod get pulled in the water by a fish and Mark goes in after it. He gets tangled in the line and started to drown. Mom jumps in, and a bear on the other bank jumps in and picks up Mark and carries him to shore. Mom picks up a fish and tosses it to the bear. The bear goes back in the woods."

"Now that is really weird...and unbelievable."

"Saw it with my own eyes."

"Anyway, Amyra goes on to tell me that Mom had the ability to transcend space and time through the use of portals. She said that Mom's Twin Flame, Mark, could move inter-dimensionally, which is why he could get around as he did. I guess he just quit trying after Mom died."

"So let me get this straight. You're telling me that my grandparents were some kind of super-humans that traveled through time? And what the hell is a Twin Flame, some sort of secret organization?"

"No, a Twin Flame is a term for two people that were conjoined souls that were separated at birth so they could experience separate lives here on earth until it was time for them to reunite.

They reunite for the betterment of the planet and usually have some mission to fulfill."

"So they are actually like superheroes."

"Sort of, but not exactly. I imagine there is some mention of a Master Bennie in Mark's book?"

"Oh yeah, an Asian master," he said sarcastically.

"Don't be so easy to dismiss what you don't understand. Amyra spoke of this Master Bennie as her twin brother, and they were here to guide, teach and assist your grandparents when needed."

"He was described by Big Guy in a *Matrix Reloaded* fashion."

"Yeah, that sounds about right."

"So why are you telling me all this now, Dad?"

"In case you need the information later, and I'm not here to provide it."

"Oh, you'll be around for the next hundred years or so. After all, we come from some pretty good lineage."

"Yeah, but unfortunately we are not immortal, at least in the physical sense."

"So, I was talking with your Nan the other night, and she said to tell you…"

"Nan. You were talking to Nan. You have been looking tired lately. Are you off your nut?"

"No, I figured out, mathematically how to open a portal."

"You what?"

"You heard what I said."

"Now I know you're off your gourd."

"No, and I will show you how I did it. I figured you wouldn't just take my word for it.

But anyway, she asked me to tell you that you will need to be prepared to handle your new son, as he will have a lot of the abilities, such as inter-dimensional travel, which Mark had. He is, in fact, one-half of a set of Twin Flames."

"Great. Now I not only have to deal with a demented father but a newborn that can travel at will. Great, just great. How am I going to explain this to Amy?"

"She'll get used to it. She's a special girl, certainly not a wuss."

"Okay, Dr. Who. Show me your stuff."

Dad put down his glass, sat back and breathed deeply. The next thing I saw was a small cloud that started to swirl with its center growing larger until we were engulfed in it.

"Hold my hand," said Dad.

We entered the vortex, going deeper and deeper until we came to a place of stillness, beauty and green grass…a meadow.

"Where in the hell are we?"

"Somewhere else," is all Dad said.

As I looked beyond my unfamiliar surroundings, I saw two people coming toward us with familiar faces. "It's Nan and Big Guy!" I cried running toward them hugging and kissing them. "I have really missed you! Where are we? Heaven?"

"No Sonny. We are just in another dimension that is parallel to your own. I see that Vinnie had to prove to you that this kind of travel was possible, Mr. Missouri. Mark and I simply learned how to do all this by walking out on faith, but with you mathematicians, I guess it takes more proofs."

"Well, you have to admit, it is a little far-fetched."

"Only if you keep your head inside the box."

"I hear we have a great-grandchild on the way," said Mark, "He's going to be quite a handful."

"That's what Dad was just telling me. I hope I am up for it."

"Oh, you'll do fine. If your Nan and I could do it, anybody can. We'll check in with you from time to time, now that you know we still exist, as you need us. We'll know when that time is. And we will return to look after the new twins when that time is right also."

"Return, as in reincarnation?"

"Yes Honey," said Nan, "We will need to guide them just like Amyra and Bennie did us."

"Them? Who's them? Are we having twins?"

"No, no. Eventually, your son will find his twin, be reunited and marry her. So don't worry, no twins."

"That's a relief. I was just getting used to the idea of having a son. I don't think I could have handled twins."

"We love you and will always be there in spirit. Light and peace to you both," they said as they faded from view.

The vortex reappeared, and we walked back through the portal. As the cloud dissipated, I realized that we were, once again, on the back porch.

Bedazzled, I said, "I think I've had enough scotch for one day. Bojangles?"

"Yeah son, Bojangles. Why don't you give Billy a call to see if he wants to join us? I'm sure he is ready for a change of scenery by now."

Chapter Seven

*A*ntonio Marcus Banos was born without fanfare, right on schedule two months later. With blonde hair like Amy's and brown eyes like mine, Mom remarked how she thought that he resembled Nan with his coloring and features.

Amy was a natural at being a great mom. I was doing good for a Banos, not great at diapers but superlative at taking naps with Tony. Elva helped out a lot, giving Amy time to rest in between feedings.

"Can you take him for a while, Sonny," said Amy, "I'm bushed."

"Sure, Honey. Come here, big boy."

But before I could reach out to get him, he popped into my arms.

"Whoa there, big fellow. I could have dropped you."

"Sonny, be more careful," Amy shouted from the next room.

"It wasn't me, it was…"

"Who? Who was it? I don't see anybody else," postpartum Amy said as she came back in the living room.

"Never mind, I will be more careful."

I watched as Amy headed back to the bedroom.

I thought, *"Oh, shit. He's already started to develop his abilities, and he's still breastfeeding. How am I going to explain this one to Amy? Oh shit. Where'd he go?"*

I found him laying on the floor next to the TV, just as Amy again returned to the living room. *"Okay,"* I thought, *"a man after my own heart."*

"Sonny! Why is Tony lying on the floor? Can't you hold him for one minute?"

"But I...never mind."

Amy just glared at me as she returned to the other room.

This is going to be harder than I thought. Maybe I can reason with him. If he's that advanced, perhaps he can understand me.

"Tony, look at me a minute."

Tony looked toward me.

"Come back over here."

Next thing you know Tony was on my lap.

"Well, will you look at that!"

I started to try to reason with him.

"You know this is a little different for me. I mean, people usually don't have babies that can move the way that you do. If you don't listen to me and just go where you want to, you will likely get hurt. That's why there is a Mom and a Dad to teach you what's safe to do and what's not. Understand?"

Tony just cooed.

"We have got to get to know one another. So, if you just trust your mom and me to help you make better decisions, it will help you get along better down here. I will teach you how to play baseball, and get you karate lessons because Big Guy insisted that if I had a kid, to make sure he took karate, and I will teach you to sail..."

"No, hell no, never!" interjected Amy as she came back into the room.

"How long have you been standing there?" I said.

"Pretty much the whole time," said Amy. "Why?"

"Oh, nothing."

"Nothing huh? Did you teach Tony to fly already?"

"Fly? I not sure what you mean."

"Don't play dumb with me. You told Tony to come to you when he was lying on the floor, and then he was in your arms. You didn't move. What's going on?"

"Well, I guess it's time we had a long talk. You are not going to believe what I am going to tell you, but it's true. Why don't I put Tony down for a nap, and we can talk about it."

"Why don't you just tell Tony to go to bed?"

"Don't be facetious."

But, before I could hardly get the words out of my mouth, Tony disappeared. We ran to his crib, where we found him curled up ready for his nap sucking on his pacifier.

"Okay, Lucy, splane!" said Amy impatiently.

"Alright, this might take a while."

"Well, I not going anywhere, unlike Jr. Jetson."

So, I told Amy everything that Dad had revealed to me, along with some of the stories that Big Guy had told me to write in his memoirs.

After I finished, Amy said, "No wonder you Banos' drink so much scotch! Jeez! I always knew you and your family were a little wackamo, but this is way off the radar. Well, I said for better or worse, and I meant it. Are you ready to go where no man has gone before, Captain Quirk?"

"Yep, beam me up, Scotty."

"I will if you fuck this up."

Shocked I said, "Dad said you won't no wuss."

"Did he say that?" poking her chest out, "Well, he be right. Let's do this!"

DAD AND MOM came back down a couple of months later to meet Tony. This time, they flew into Raleigh, so I drove to the airport to pick them up.

Seeing them come through the terminal, I waved my hand and said, "Hi Guys! How was your flight?"

"Hi Sonny," both yelled as we exchanged hugs.

"These flights are really tiring for me now," said Dad.

"Yes, it did seem longer than usual," said Mom. "Vinnie, we need to run down and get our baggage."

"I'll run down and get the bags," I said. "You guys look bushed," noticing that Dad was looking unusually ashen.

"Thanks, Sonny," said Dad.

After pulling the car around and getting everyone on board, I said, "Are you guys hungry? There are plenty of places to grab a bite here, but not so many on the trip back."

"I'm a little hungry, but I'm ready to get to New Bern to see my new grandson," Dad beamed.

"I can't wait for you to meet Tony. He is so...well like you and I talked about Dad."

"What'd he tell you Honey," asked Angel, "that he was going to have a big dick?"

"Angel! I never..." said Vinnie.

"Caught you off guard that time, didn't I? Gotta keep you on your toes."

"Yeah, and I need to keep me on the highway," I said laughing, tears rolling down both cheeks.

Arriving at THE home in New Bern, THE parents got to meet THE baby.

Amy greeted us at the door with Tony in her arms.

"Hi, everybody. Come in, come in! This is Tony."

"Well, hello big boy. Come to your Gram," said Angel, holding out her arms.

And Tony was in her arms. He just smiled up at Mom and cooed.

"What...just happened?"

"Y'all might wanna sit down, and we'll try to explain. You wanna drink?"

"Yes, I think so, maybe scotch," said Angel.

Vinnie was looking over at Tony and then back to me said, "Yes son scotch, lots of scotch."

"Okay Sonny, I think it's time you let your mom in on what went on the last time we were down here and reveal what Big Guy and Nan told you," said Vinnie.

"Big Guy and Nan? Are you off your nut? How?" asked Angel.

"Patience Mom, it's kind of a long story."

"Better make mine a double," said Angel.

After everyone got comfortable, and of course, I fixed myself a drink, I once again began to tell the tale of Dad and me going through the portal.

Tony just cooed in Mom's lap as I revealed everything that Big Guy and Nan had explained to me about Tony's future before the baby was born.

"I know what I have just told you borders on a 1950's B Sci-Fi movie," I said. "Hell, it's hard for Amy and me to believe it. But you are just going to have to believe what I say on faith, without me going into the how part because, to be honest, it is just too hard to explain. But, you hold the proof in your lap."

"So, a typical Banos," chided Angel, swaying just a little from the scotch. "Oh, they're not so tough," she said tickling Tony underneath his chin.

"Yeah, pretty tough," I said, "but I think Tony and I have come to an understanding, which makes it easier."

"You have reasoned with a two-month-old?"

"Not just any two-month-old, and he knows what we tell him is for his own good."

"Well, that just makes perfect sense, doesn't it, dear?" said Angel as the scotch and the sarcasm began to glow brighter in her face. "You could have let me in on this little revelation, you know. There have been enough surprises for me as of late."

"I'm sorry," said Vinnie quietly, "it just slipped my mind with us winding down the business and all."

"Winding down the business? When did this happen?"

"We just decided that it was time for us to retire and live out the rest of our lives together without the hassle of running a business. It was time, so we sold it."

"I guess that does make sense, and maybe now you can visit the baby and us more often."

"I sure hope so," said Vinnie.

Angel said, "I guess we had better get unpacked while I can still move."

Amy responded, "You two go ahead, and I will fix you a quick snack to hold you over before dinner."

Mom and Dad went upstairs with their bags as Amy fixed snacks. Tony and I did what Tony and I do best, catch a few z's on the couch.

As Amy arrived with a platter of fruit, cheese, and crackers, she sarcastically said, "Thanks for watching Dad, Tony."

"Wha...I was just resting my eyes. Those snacks look great!"

"Hands off, Mr. Banos," she said playfully smacking my fingers, "wait for your mom and dad to come back downstairs."

Mom and Dad soon reappeared to join us.

"Thank you," said Angel, "I was beginning to get famished. Oh, this is so good," as she nibbled on some of the cheese and crackers."

"Would you like something else to drink?"

"Yes, but not scotch. Do you have some of that wonderful sauvignon blanc?"

"Of course!" said Amy returning to the kitchen to get some glasses and some wine.

"I believe I would just like some water if that is okay with you Sonny," said Vinnie.

"Sure Dad, I'll get it for you."

Vinnie said, "Sonny after we eat our snack and rest a bit, why don't we take a ride down to the marina. I'd like to take a look at the boats."

"You're not thinking of buying one are you?"

"Oh, no," said Vinnie laughing, "just want to do a little reminiscing and smell the salt air."

"Sure, let me know when you're ready. I have a clear schedule today."

"Except, when it's your turn for baby duty, or should I say *baby doody*," said Amy.

"Yeah, yeah," I said moaning.

"I'll help with the doody duties while you are gone," said Angel.

"Thanks, Mom."

After we ate our snack and visited a little while longer, Dad and I drove down to the marina. He was unusually quiet. Dad just rode, looking out the window, deep in his thoughts.

Once we pulled into the marina, he spotted the old *Karli Anna*. Someone had bought it years ago, but it was good to see her in such excellent shape.

"Lot of memories aboard that craft," said Dad, "good and bad."

"Yeah, good and bad," I said reflecting on capsizing the boat, trying to impress Amy.

Then Dad started to look around at the other boats, walking up and down the docks until he came to a bench. There he said, "Let's have a seat. I've got something to tell you."

The sound of his voice took on a serious tone. He usually didn't give serious talks anymore. I was beginning to feel a little like I was 15 again, waiting for the dolling out of punishment.

"Sure Dad, what's up?"

Plopping down, he breathed a deep sigh and began, "Sonny, I have evidently been sick for a while now. I didn't realize how sick I was until recently. I had been weak, sure, but shrugged it off as just getting older. But, then, I went in for a checkup. Last week the doctor got my blood results back. It wasn't good. I have stage four colon cancer."

"Oh no, Dad," I said tearing up.

"The doctor said that if I don't have surgery, I will only have about six months. But even if I do have the surgery, I will only make it about eighteen. Either way, it's not good."

By now my tears are flowing. All of the joy and happiness that had surrounded us in these last few months came to a screeching halt.

"Have you gotten a second opinion."

"Oh yes, and a third. There are no other options left. At least, I have time to get my affairs in order and get to see my grandson and share some time with you and Amy. And of course, drink some scotch."

"Yes Dad, and drink some scotch," I uttered as my voice trailed off.

After a moment of silence, I asked, "When do you have to go in for the surgery."

"As soon as I get back. I'll have to wear a damn colostomy bag from now on, however long that is."

"Can you still eat some Carolina barbecue?" I jested, trying to lighten the conversation.

"Hell son, I can eat anything. Does it make a shit?" Dad said, sounding a bit more like Big Guy than Dad.

"Yeah, but can you take a shit?" I retorted.

"Wearing my bag, I can take a shit and leave a shit anytime and anywhere I want."

"Who gives a shit?" we both said, laughing uncontrollably.

We laughed 'til we cried and then started laughing again. Calming down, Dad said, "Let's go back to the house if you don't mind. I want to spend a little more time with Superman. You are going to have your hands full with that one," he said as he patted me on the back and walked me to the car.

I got the call a few weeks later. While Dad had made it through the surgery, the cancer had spread throughout his body. A blood clot had lodged in his pulmonary artery and in his weakened state, he died the next day. I was overwhelmed with grief; we all were.

We all thought that he would at least be around for the next year. He made it a month to the day from the last time he came down to visit us.

Amy and I flew to Toronto. Billy and Elva kept the baby. I warned him not to try any of his shenanigans on them as they would not be prepared to deal with them. I just hoped he understood.

We rented a car at the airport and drove to Mom and Dad's home. Now, that would undoubtedly take some getting used to...Mom's home. She greeted us warmly. I know she was glad to see us, but she was still in a daze, not quite knowing what to do with herself. We tried to be kind and light-hearted, but we all had severe tonnage in the chest area.

The funeral was pre-arranged, which made the process much more bearable. We all were in this twilight sleep, not dwelling with reality and yet knowing that this was it. We'd never see Dad again.

Too many funerals, way too soon. Nan's I had just about gotten over. Big Guy's had not been that long ago, but I was more prepared for it. We spent a lot of time together before he died. But this...this was much more devastating. I expected my Dad to help me raise Tony, to help me teach him as he taught me. Now, it was just up to me...up to me.

The funeral was inaudible. I don't remember a single word because I didn't hear a single word. A million and one things filled my mind that my Dad had told me, that I didn't want to forget; the memories that I didn't want to lose nor did I want to lose the memory of the face of my dad. *That* I wished to have permanently etched in my mind. These were the only things that mattered on this day...the only things.

As we were leaving the gravesite, I noticed an elderly gentleman in the back of the crowd that I didn't recognize. We headed for the limousines and drove off, while he just stood there by the grave like a sentinel.

We, then, went back to Mom's house, where a huge crowd of Mom and Dad's friends had gathered to eat food, drink and share remembrances. It was good to hear his friends share stories about my dad. This, more than anything, started to lift me from my funk.

I had decided to go back to the cemetery, alone, to pay my final respects. When I arrived, the old gentleman was still at the grave. Curious, I approached him. As I did, I noticed he was not just an old man, but an old Asian man. He finally looked up and said, "Hello Sonnysan, I am Master Bennie, a friend of your grandfather. We have much to talk about."

Chapter Eight

"THE Master Bennie?"

"The only one I know."

"How can you still be alive? My grandfather said you were much older than him, and he died a several years ago at 93."

"I don't know, I guess good things last," said Bennie laughing.

"I suppose."

"You are a lot like him, impetuous. Got to know why clock work, not happy that it just keep time."

"Why are you here? Did you know my Dad?"

"Aye, know much. You not so much, but you learn if you listen."

"I don't know that I am in the mood for listening today. My dad just died, and I only have my thoughts on him and my family right now."

"Understand, we talk later before you leave. We do have much to discuss."

"Give me your number, and I will call you once things have settled down a little."

"Number? I have no number. You no worry. I find you when you ready."

I turned toward Dad's grave and then looked back to find that Master Bennie had disappeared. Maybe, he was just in my imagination. Maybe.

Amy greeted me as I headed up the steps to Mom's house.

"How'd it go? You okay?"

"Yeah, I'm fine. How is Mom doing."

"She's fine right now. Seems to be enjoying her friends that have stopped by."

"I'm more worried about how she's going to be once they stop coming."

"Yeah, I know. I got a call from my mom and dad, and they said that Jr. Jetson said to say, 'Hello' and that he would be happy to fly up and join us if we wanted him to...just kidding. Everything is fine, and Tony seems to be behaving himself."

"Good. I don't need anything else to worry about right now."

"Come in and let me fix you a plate. I know you didn't eat anything before you left."

"That would be great. I am starting to get a little hungry."

Putting her arm around me, she walked me inside. I don't know how I would have made it through this if it wasn't for the love of Amy surrounding me. I leaned over and kissed her on the forehead as we entered the hallway. An all-knowing smile pursed her lips as she continued to the kitchen.

The next morning, everyone slept in late. We had had a full day of it yesterday, and now it was time to start the daunting task of cleaning up. I went downstairs to start some coffee only to find a small miracle had occurred. Instead of seeing a dirty kitchen with leftovers on the counter, I found a spotless one with all of the leftover food neatly put up in the refrigerator and coffee brewing. How in the world did this happen? Just then, a couple appeared in maid and butler attire and said, "Good Morning sir."

"Good Morning," I said. "I didn't know Mom had a staff."

"We were hired by the people who catered. I hope we didn't disturb you."

"No, not at all. Thank you very much. This will mean so much to my mother."

"Good, we try to do our best. Is there anything else we can do to help you?"

"No, thank you."

"Then we will be off."

And they left out the front door. I followed behind them a few seconds later to see them off and offer them a tip, but there was no one in sight. Odd...I thought.

When Mom and Amy came downstairs, they couldn't believe their eyes.

"Oh, Sonny. Did you clean all of this up for us?"

Laughing, I said, "I wish I could take the credit. It was the maid and butler that the caterer had hired. They did it all."

Mom had a puzzled stare on her face as she said, "But we didn't hire a caterer. All of our friends brought the food and drink."

She then quietly sat down, deep in thought.

"Well, there has to be an explanation," said Amy. "Maybe one of your friends hired them."

"But how did they get in?"

"I don't know, but here's a card that they left on the counter. Hmmm...Hana Valet Services, but there's no number or address on the card. That's strange."

Almost giggling, Mom said, "Oh, not so strange...not so strange at all."

———

"Look, after we eat some breakfast, do you two think you would be okay for a couple of hours. I need to go out for awhile."

"I'm sure we can manage," said Mom. "You go ahead, Sonny. Call us if you're going to be too late."

After wolfing down a bagel and swilling some orange juice, I said, "I will call you if I am going to be out late, so you guys won't worry."

"Okay Sonny, be careful," said Angel.

"I will Mom. I love you. Bye Amy," I said as I gently placed a kiss on her forehead.

"Bye, Dear," she said as she squeezed my hand.

I left, really not knowing where I was heading, but I had a feeling that the Master would find me. Sure enough, as I was rounding the corner, there sat Master Bennie on a park bench.

"Hello, Sonnysan. Beautiful day."

"Hello, it is a beautiful day, and it is even more beautiful knowing that I didn't have to clean up that mess this morning."

"And what mess was that?"

"The mess from yesterday's wake. Someone showed our family a great deal of love and kindness by cleaning up everything."

"Yes, I suppose someone did. Did you thank them?"

"Thank you."

"Why thank me? Did you see me?"

"Oh, I don't know how, but I think I did."

"Ah, maybe now you are ready to listen with heart and not eyes. Eyes deceive, heart never."

"So, what do I need to hear?"

"God's voice, my son. Look at the trees and listen to what they tell you. Listen to the small whisper of the wind, but not with ears, with heart. Heart guide you, not mind. You have analytical mind that you need to turn off so you can experience those things not easily seen."

"Like when my dad took me into the portal?"

"Aye, but this caused his illness. He knew the mathematics involved to invoke the portal, but he was unaware of the dangers. That is why I am here. You have much ahead of you, but you need a guide to keep you safe."

"What do you mean, caused his illness?"

"Portals are very harmful to the human body, especially if that body is not trained in such things. Each time a portal is used for time and space travel, there is stress on the body. Even a superhuman, such as your grandmother could only pass through three times. The third time she contracted leukemia and was in a coma for three days. But she was able to recover quickly and heal because she was different than you or your dad. She used it a fourth time to save your grandfather, and she died because of it. Your dad used it two times and contracted colon cancer which he could not overcome."

"So why are you here telling me all of this?"

"Because I do not want you to make the same mistake. As you have already noticed, your son Tony is not like you. He already has inter-dimensional travel abilities. He is like Mark, your grandfather, able to move from one dimension to another at will. Unlike Mark, he does not have to train to have this ability. However, he will need your and Amy's guidance to keep his abilities secret until it is time for him to use them. You must help him to shed his ego so that his powers will be used for good, as they were intended."

"Intended for what? When?"

"That will be revealed to you when it is time. Right now, you need to help Tony to grow in the right ways as any normal boy would. He is one-half of himself right now and eventually will reunite with his twin as Mark did. Then, they will complete their mission."

"What mission?"

"Don't know yet, not time. All I do know is that this is not usually the way the universe does this reuniting of twins. There are usually twin mentors to help them. This time, it's different. The mentors are late, as expected, so you and Amy will just have to do."

"So the universe made a mistake?"

"No, universe never makes mistake, it's just different this time. We adjust."

"What do we have to do?"

"Protect, care for and instruct Tony."

"I'm not sure I know what to do? And who is the other twin?"

"Don't know yet, but she'll be around. You help her too."

"How can I help someone when I don't know who they are?"

"You'll know. Listen with heart and give love. Love is the answer to all things. Love is your salvation and your weapon. Use it always in all things. Never let anger, grief or revenge overcome you. Love really does conquer all," said Bennie as he faded from view.

"What the hell?"

I looked around, and he was gone. What did he mean? How will I explain this to Amy?

I sat there on the bench for a long while, reflecting on what the old man had told me, then headed for the house. Upon entering, Mom greeted me and asked, "Did you have a nice chat with Master Bennie?"

"What? How did you know?"

"Bennie has been looking in on our affairs for a great many years. He was your grandfather's mentor. He is a spirit being and not tied to time or space. He always appears when he is needed, and only then. If he met with you, it must be of great importance."

"So you know this guy?"

"He showed up when your grandmother died. He helped your dad get through the loss of his mother and showed up again when Mark passed on. He guided us in our financial affairs after Mark's death, never making recommendations, but asking questions through which we found the answers as to what needed to be done. And then he would disappear. He's the one that put it in our head that you might be better off living with your grandparents in New Bern, knowing full well that that was where you were to meet and marry Amy. Like he always said, *"Me know much, you not so much."* Grinning she continued, "When your dad got sick he came back to help us get through some difficult decisions."

"So, you know what happened to Dad."

"Yes, It's one of those things you get used to being married to a Banos. I'm at peace with it. When you found the card this morning on the counter, I knew he was nearby. Has he talked to you about Tony?"

"Yes, how did you know?"

"Oh, he came to talk to me and your dad, not long ago, after we returned from Carolina this past time. He explained what was going to happen in Tony's life. Anna and Mark will return to help him later, but for right now, you and Amy will have to take on the load."

"What do you mean Anna and Mark will return? And who is Anna?"

"Anna Sopoulos is your grandmother's real name. She changed it while in witness protection to Sopie. Mark actually is Thomas Marcus Banos, which is why your first name is Thomas. They were twin flames, like Tony and whoever he is to reunite with. They will eventually come back to guide them on their journey, just like Master Bennie and Sister Amyra did your grandparents."

"Have you told Amy any of this?"

"She's told me everything," said Amy coming downstairs.

"And you're okay with all this?"

"Don't be such a Dabb. Why wouldn't I be? It's what we have to do."

"Don't keep calling me a Dabb."

"Dumb Ass Banos Boy," Amy taunted.

Angel said, "That's what Master Bennie always called you guys. I think the shoe fits!"

She had me again, caught with my mouth open, just waiting for the flies to land.

Mom just giggled and said, "She has a mother's heart. She'll know what her son needs."

"Speaking of our son," said Amy, "I guess it's time we get ready to head back and see what P-Dabb's been up to."

"Oh, come on now! Really?"

"Oh, I think it's kinda cute," said Mom.

"Are you going to be alright, Mom?"

"Yes, Sonny, I going to be fine. Go do what you have to do now."

Chapter Nine

*W*e arrived to find *P-Dabb*, as Amy now called him, nestled with Billy in the easy chair in the den. Both were sleeping soundly and snoring loudly with the TV showing another *Law and Order* rerun that had them both enthralled.

"Typical Banos. I can see that I have my work cut out for me," said Amy.

Elva, cutting off the TV, said, "Time to wake up. Tony's got to go home."

"Wha...what? Oh, I was just resting my eyes while Tony took a nap. Hi, y'all. How was your flight."

"Long," I said, "we are glad to be back home."

"Yes, thank you, Mom and Dad, for taking care of our little P-Dabb while we were gone," said Amy. "I never had to worry about him as long as I knew you two were looking after him."

"Oh, he was no bother at all. He just stayed where we were and didn't cry once," said Elva. "Funny though, he sure does manage to keep up with us. I'm not sure whether he crawls really fast or we have just gotten so old and slow."

"Yeah, and he's developed a real taste for blue crab," said Billy laughing. You may have to wean him off of those before he goes back to baby food."

"He's eating real food already? He doesn't have any teeth yet."

"Yeah, but he likes to eat. Poor critter has to gum it to death, though. I know how he feels."

Once back home, we unpacked and then proceeded to feed Tony his supper. Looking at us like we had lost our minds and then looking at his plate with baby food on it, he uttered, "Cwab."

Amy and I just looked at each other and looked back at P-Dabb.

"His first word is *cwab*. Isn't that precious."

"Cwack cwab," he said again smacking his fist on the plate two times.

"I think he wants to cwack, I mean crack crabs. Billy said he ate them, but he didn't tell me he cracked them, too."

"What'll we do? We just got home, and we don't have any crabs here."

"I'll call Dad and see what he did."

"Dad," said Amy with a slight bit of exasperation, "what did you do to Tony? He won't eat his supper and keeps saying *Crack Crabs.*"

"I told you he had developed a taste for crab, and I don't know how, but he learned to crack the shells and get the meat. He can almost do it as good as I can."

"But we don't have any crab. We just got back, and he is getting fussy."

"He tried that crap with me when we were having something other than crab one night. I explained to him that he couldn't eat crab every day, it would give him gout. Funny, he seemed to understand me. So, I offered him a Vienna sausage and some corn pone, and he did fine. But, if you want some crab, I have some left that you are welcome to."

"I think Vienna sausages will be just fine for now. I guess he has already graduated from the baby food and he doesn't even have teeth."

"Yep. Me neither. Call me if you need me."

"Okay Dad, I will," Amy said as she hung up and looked in Tony's direction.

"Okay, P-Dabb," said Amy, "just like Pop-Pop said, you can't eat crab every day. Today, it's Vienna sausages," handing him a new plate.

Tony just smiled and started eating the sausages.

"Hey, little fellow. We missed you so much," I said, reflecting upon my Dad's gentle touch with me when I was little.

After dinner, we played with Tony on the floor for a while and then Amy said, "Time for bed P-Dabb."

I guess she was going to make it stick. A daily reminder of my heritage. Nice.

I decided to get Nan's diary back out and see what she had written about Dad. I scoured the entries that she wrote during her time in Carol Stream, to grasp a little of what he was like as a child, basking in every detail that I could uncover. I continued to read how he was a little daredevil, running Nan ragged at times. How he loved to play outside, especially with the golf set Mark had gotten him for Christmas. Funny how she and Mark almost got back together when she lived in Carol Stream. He even asked her to marry him without even knowing it was the girl he fell in love with so many years before. She said yes, of course, but she knew it was her *Tom*. She must have been so afraid, taking care of my dad while being in witness protection for all of those years. Then, she put her son's life before her own, moving to New Orleans to escape a hitman, knowing she could never tell Mark where she was going or why...*A mother's heart.*

"Well, I finally got our Jr. Jetson off to sleep. He is so sweet. I really missed him."

"Me, too."

"What 'cha doing?"

"Oh, I was just reading some entries in Nan's diary to learn a little about my Dad growing up."

"That's nice. I am sure there is a lot you don't know about his childhood."

"You can say that again. They lived in the witness protection program throughout his high school years."

"Really?"

"Yeah, and Big Guy didn't come back in the picture until they had already settled in New Orleans. He ended up teaching at Holy Cross down there, and my dad played in the marching band as a sophomore. He didn't know Dad was Nan's son and they totally met by accident, just as Big Guy told me in his memoirs. See…?"

Amy looked at the entries about Nan hearing someone shout behind her in the hospital corridor. It was Big Guy holding a rose.

"How romantic," Amy said.

"Yeah, hard to imagine Big Guy romantic," I said laughing.

"Well, then it says some personal things about that evening when they get back together, that I think I will just skip over," Amy continued. "I just don't feel right."

"Understood."

"Awww…then they go to see your Dad, who is in the hospital getting his wisdom teeth extracted and ask his permission for them to get married. Nan calls your dad her little chipmunk."

"Isn't that sweet," I said sarcastically.

Punching me, Amy said, "After your dad healed up, it looks like they took a mini-vacation to Gulfport. I see, by these entries, where the Banos Boys love for fishing came from."

"Let me see. Wow, Dad landed a huge Spanish Mackerel on his first fishing trip! I can't wait to take Tony fishing."

"As long as it's not on a sailboat."

"Never gonna let me live that down, are you?"

"Nope. No never."

"As expected."

"This trip down memory lane is fascinating, but I'm getting tired. Let's get ready for bed."

"Sounds great to me. Grrr…"

"To SLEEP."

"Oh."

MONTHS PASSED by and I took up a new hobby...golf. I wasn't much good at it, but it took the edge off my memories of Dad. I didn't realize it at the time, but I was depressed. I had a newborn son and all the responsibilities that come with that, plus the added responsibilities due to who he was to become. Amy was great. She took care of everything, and I mean everything. My wife was Supermom. Amy had taken a year's leave from the institute so she could spend extra time nurturing Tony. She watched the baby, did the laundry, cooked the meals, cleaned the house and cut the yard. I played golf, before work, at lunch, sometimes after work. It had become an all-consuming obsession. I think I thought I could make it into the PGA if I just played one more round each day.

One Saturday, as I was loading the clubs into the trunk, Amy said, "Why don't you take P-Dabb with you. I'm sure he would enjoy the fresh air," as she loaded the stroller into the trunk.

"Oh, okay."

"Here's his diaper bag."

"Am I going to need that?"

"I believe you might, Mr. Jackoff Nichol-ass," she said with unbelievable constraint.

As I started to get in the car, Amy said, "Here you might need this as well."

"What?"

Looking up, she dangled Tony in the air.

"Oh, yeah. Sorry."

Fastening Tony in his car seat, we took off for the course.

I did fine with Tony in tow. He seemed to enjoy the sunshine. And then, he began a familiar grunting.

"Oh shit, Tony, we have only played three holes."

I placed his blanket on the fairway and began the task of cleaning him up and reinstalling the clean diaper.

"Play through," I yelled at the group behind me.

Laughing, one of the other golfers said, "Looks like you got a big bogey on that hole."

"Very funny," I retorted.

I picked Tony up and put him in his stroller and handed him his pacifier, which he sucked on until he fell asleep. Now, I thought, I can get a little golf in. We strolled to the next hole with Tony still fast asleep. I took a swing. It was a beautiful drive, at least 350 yards. As I was admiring my stroke, I almost had one...Tony and his stroller were rolling down the fairway toward the water hazard.

"Oh my God! Help!" I yelled, but there was no one in sight. I ran down the fairway to head off the impending disaster, tackling the stroller before it hit the water. It overturned, waking Tony, who started crying.

"I'm so sorry," I said as I started to cry. As I picked Tony up, I noticed his arm go limp.

"Oh God, his arm is broken!"

I rushed back up to the clubhouse, to my car and sped out heading for Carteret General. Stupid ass me, I must've forgotten to lock the wheels on the stroller. Carrying Tony into the ER, I got a nurse's attention who quickly took us back for X-rays. The X-rays confirmed my greatest fear, his arm was broken. The doctor questioned me as to how this had happened, and I sheepishly explained the circumstances.

Shaking his head, the doctor said, "Wait here while I prepare a cast. Poor little fellow."

Coming back about fifteen minutes later, Tony had stopped crying. He was just sitting on my lap resting. Then the doctor said, "Put him on the table so I can start to put the cast on."

With unbearable agony, I laid Tony on the table, but when I let go of him, he reached up for me with both arms.

The doctor said in astonishment, "What the hell? How can he reach up if his arm is broken? Nurse, take this boy back and have that arm X-rayed again."

This time the results showed no signs of a break.

"Let's X-ray his arm one more time. There has to be an error somewhere. That first film definitely showed a simple fracture."

But the third X-ray showed the same results, no breaks, anywhere.

"This beats all I have ever seen. Tony is one lucky boy. Mr. Banos, I surely hope you are more careful in the future. This could have ended up a lot worse."

"Oh, I will be. From now on, I will be the Dad that I am supposed to be."

Upon arriving home that evening, Amy said, "Did you boys play nice."

"Sure did," kissing Amy on the cheek.

"Honey, where are your clubs?"

"Oh, I gave them away. I don't have time for golf anymore. It's time to be a Dad."

Chapter Ten

*I*n the blink of an eye, Jr. Jetson had turned six and was ready for his first day of school. Neither Amy nor I were quite as prepared but fell into the routine soon enough. His kindergarten teacher, Ms. Cutright, was energetic and vibrant, yet stern and we warned Tony not to pull any of his shenanigans in her class. We enrolled Tony in the Epiphany School of Global Studies, which was founded by Nicholas Sparks, a famous novelist and an old fishing buddy of my grandfather, Mark. Nick's great-granddaughter, Jodi was in Tony's class, and the two soon became inseparable. With her hazel eyes and blonde hair, folks could have easily mistaken her for Amy's daughter.

Tony came running in the door as Amy brought him home from school.

"Hey Champ, where's the fire?" I asked.

"Sorry Dad, I was just excited to be home."

"So how do you like going to school, Tony?" I inquired.

"It's great. Today Ms. Cutright told us that if we were good the rest of the year, she would give us ice cream sandwiches to eat when the school year ends."

"That sounds good. Ms. Cutright seems to be such a nice teacher."

"Oh, she is but," Tony continued, "I'm not sure if I am really going to like that though. I can't imagine putting ice cream on bread."

Amy had just walked in at the end of the conversation.

Laughing she said, "I guess we never bought any ice cream sandwiches before, so you don't know what to expect. It is just vanilla ice cream between two chocolate cookies so you can eat it with your hands and not get messy. They are mmm... good!"

"Okay! That does sound good. I can't wait 'til the end of the year."

"Well, maybe next time when I am at the store I can get some for you to try."

"Yay!" we both shouted.

"Mom, today we learned how to finger paint. See the flower I made for you?"

"Oh, it's beautiful! Thank you so much."

"Jodi made her mom one too. It was really pretty."

"You and Jodi have become such good friends. Why don't I call her mom and see if she would like to come over this Saturday and maybe the three of us can bake some cookies?"

"That would be great, Mom! Can you call her now?"

"Okay. Let me get the number."

After a few minutes, Seneca Sparks picked up the phone.

"Hello?"

"Hi, this is Amy Banos, Tony's mom."

"Oh hi, how are you?"

"Fine. I was just wondering if maybe Jodi would like to come over Saturday and play with Tony."

"Oh, I think that would be a great idea. She talks about him all the time."

"Great! I would love to finally meet you. Say maybe 11:00?"

"Sounds great. See you then. Goodbye."

"Goodbye."

"Tony, Jodi is going to come over Saturday."

"Yay!" cried Tony as he ran upstairs to his room.

Saturday came, and Seneca arrived with Jodi at eleven. The kids took off to Tony's room as Amy offered Seneca a cup of coffee.

"I'm going to town to pick up some things," I said. "Do you need anything?"

"No, I can't think of anything."

"Seneca, this is my husband, Sonny."

"Howdy," I said, " you must be Jodi's mom."

"That would be me," grinned Seneca.

"Well, gotta get going before the day gets behind me. I will see y'all later. Nice to meet you, Seneca."

"Nice to meet you, too, Sonny."

"Well, this is nice," Seneca said as Amy poured her a cup of coffee. "Usually on Saturdays, it's run to the store and run home to do the laundry. No time for a leisurely cup of coffee."

"I know what you mean," said Amy sighing. "And now with Tony in school, it just seems like there is never enough time to breathe let alone actually do anything fun."

"I know what you mean. Can you believe the kids are already learning to write in cursive? I am so glad that Ms. Cutright is going back to teaching that. They discouraged it for so many years. But I am still surprised that she teaches it in kindergarten."

"Yeah, Tony was having difficulty with it at first, but now it's just old hat to him."

"You know, going back to having fun, maybe I have an idea. Since the kids love playing together so much, why don't we create some Mom and Dad playtime as well? Do you like playing games or cards?"

"Sonny and I both adore playing Rook."

"Oh, that is one of my favorites! Let's plan on getting together next week at my house. I'm sure Gabriel and Sonny will hit it off."

"Sounds like a well-made plan to me. Let's do it!"

"Okay! I gotta run now. What time do you want me to pick Jodi up?"

"Maybe around four?"

"Okay. See you then."

After that, the kids got together on the weekends for "play dates" at either our home or at the Sparks', and we soon began a lifelong friendship with Gabriel and Seneca playing cards almost every Saturday night.

"Would you like another glass of wine, Seneca?" inquired Amy.

"Maybe just a tad more. Gabriel has me driving tonight so I best not get too snockered."

"Well, it's your turn. I drove home last time," bristled Gabriel.

"True, true. And you are also the one who had to call a tow truck to get the car out of the ditch last time," chided Seneca.

"But it was good scotch."

"Yes, it was good scotch," I laughed.

"Maybe a little too good," interjected Amy.

"Okay, one more round of Rook and we have got to go. Your deal Amy," said Seneca.

Seneca was a stay at home mom, which really helped out since she usually picked up the kids from school while the rest of us finished up our days at work. She was a fun and outgoing person and a great fit for Amy. Seneca loved going out on the boat, catching fish with the best of us. She, too, was from Canada, of Cree descent, which made her name kind of an oxymoron. Her parents moved down to Coastal Carolina when she was about ten.

Gabriel and I got along famously and had a lot in common. We both loved to fish, and we loved to drink scotch. Two out of two ain't bad. Gabriel had followed in his grandfather's footsteps, not as a writer, but as an editor with a local publishing company, Penske Publishing, here in New Bern.

One evening, while we were sipping on some scotch and smoking panatellas on the back deck, (of course we were), I mentioned to him that my grandfather had a manuscript, and asked him if he would be interested in taking a look at it.

"I'd be happy to read through it for content. I can't promise anything, but I'd be more than happy to take a look at it."

It was then that I said, "I also have a diary that was written by my grandmother, and the entries that I have read so far seem to fill in the blanks to my grandfather's memoirs. If you like what you see, you may want to look at it as well."

"Sounds interesting, Sonny. You know, we have a few ghost-writers down at the firm that may want to tackle it. Let me read through the material, and I will let you know."

"Okay, I'll finish reading my grandmother's diary to see what else is in it that might help you."

"Sounds good. Have you guys given any thought to summer vacation this year?"

"Not yet. We have been so busy getting used to this school thing."

"I know what you mean. I just thought it might be nice if we all went somewhere together."

"Now, you know that sounds like fun. Any thoughts as to where?"

"I know this is going to sound really original," Gabriel said laughing, "but I was thinking maybe Disney World. We could get one of those all-inclusive packages and stay right there on the property."

"You know, Amy and I had talked about Disney before, and I think Tony and Jodi are old enough now that they would really enjoy it."

"Well, let me call my travel agent and see what a package would run for us all staying in one resort. Do you think we should drive or fly?"

"Fly definitely. A twelve-hour drive with two kids in tow would be miserable."

"Yeah, good point. Let's talk to the girls and see what they think."

"Honey, can you and Seneca come in here for a minute."

The girls soon joined us on the back deck.

"What are you two cooking up?" asked Amy.

"Gabriel and I were just talking and thought it would be nice if all of us went on a vacation together."

"Oh Sonny, that sounds like a great idea. What do you think, Seneca?"

"Sound great to me. Where are you two geniuses thinking of going?"

Gabriel said, "What do y'all think about going down to Disney World?"

"Oh, I think that would be wonderful," said Seneca.

"Yeah, the kids will love it," echoed Amy.

"Then Disney it is. I'll call the travel agent next week."

So we started to plan our trip, departing as soon as school was out.

LATER THAT EVENING after everyone had left, I told Amy about Gabriel reading Mark's memoirs.

"Oh, that's wonderful," said Amy, "Now maybe you'll have a chance to fulfill the promise you made to your grandfather."

"Well, one of them at least."

"What do you mean? What else did you promise him?"

"That last day, when he was with Marty, Big Guy gave him a necklace that was Nan's. He told Marty that I was to give it to my first grandson."

"Grandson?"

"Well, not today. Anyway, I have never seen Marty more adamant about anything in my life, other than his Blue Moon and old S-10. I am certain there is some reason behind it, but I just haven't been able to figure it out yet. Maybe there's a clue in this old diary. I guess I'd better get busy and finish reading Nan's diary to see if I can figure out what else can be used for the book."

SEPTEMBER 2005: The flood waters finally receded in New Orleans. Mark and I had stayed behind to help the children who were too sick to be evacuated from Charity Hospital. However, when the levees broke, the water flooded the first floor, so we had no choice but to move the children to the second floor. We, then, decided we would have to make a run for it to the Super Dome, which was being set up as an emergency shelter. We went out to the 2nd level parking garage, and a shot rang out. Thanks to Amyra's spirit, I turned just in the nick of time, and the bullet grazed my necklace. Mark literally turned himself into a fireball and killed the would-be assassin. Mark and I later found ourselves in a portal and were transported to Monroe, Louisiana, 285 miles away.

We called Agent Kroner for help, and he directed us to a local hospital. Marty and Vinnie came to pick us up. While we waited, Mark explained to me what had happened in the parking garage. I told him what I thought had happened from my perspective. This was the first time that we realized that we both had certain supernatural powers. This was also the first time that we started to understand what our Twin Flame relationship was all about.

We were pronounced dead at the hospital, for our protection, and moved to Bethesda, Maryland while Agent Kroner tried to figure out what to do with us.

"Amy, you have got to read this. This is where Big Guy's book ends. I thought it was just embellishment and dramatic effect on his part, but Nan verifies everything he said. It even goes on to explain what happened to them after they left New Orleans. That necklace that we were talking about seemed to have saved her life. Maybe that's why it is so important."

After taking a look at the entries, Amy said, "Whoa! This is some serious shit. I can hardly believe it myself, but after talking to your mom…"

"What did she say?"

"She was telling me about your dad experimenting with time travel using portals. She believes that that is how he contracted cancer."

"Yes, Master Bennie told me the same thing. They are certainly not something to play with."

I continued to say without thinking, "Look, it says here that while they were in the hospital, X-rays were taken and showed that both Big Guy and Nan had stress fractures throughout their bodies that healed in a matter of hours. That must be what happened to Tony..."

"What do you mean, happened to Tony?"

"Er, I..."

"Spill," said Amy.

"You remember when I took Tony golfing? Well, we had a little accident with the stroller, and I thought I had broken his arm. Actually, I did break his arm."

"I rushed him to the emergency room, and they did X-rays and confirmed that it was broken. But then, as they were starting to put on the cast, he reached up for me with his broken arm. So, they took more X-rays and there showed no signs of a break."

"Well, I wondered when you were going to fess up. I received a bill from the hospital shortly afterward explaining the whole thing."

"Oops."

"Yeah, oops."

"You mad."

"No, I love you, and I just figured that you having to live with this little regret and giving up golf was punishment enough. I know your dad's death was overwhelming for you and that golf was your escape. I knew you would come to deal with it in time. I just wish you had told me. You know you can tell me anything. I am your best friend...forever."

"Thanks, Amy. You really are and always have been my best friend...and lover!" I said as I picked her up in the air and spun her around. "Make up sex?"

"Oh yeah, make up sex," said Amy as we retired to the bedroom.

Chapter Eleven

"Oh shit!" I screamed as the tremors started and erupted into obnoxious laughter.

"What?" asked Amy, "What?"

"I can't..." choking back the tears and handing her the diary.

Amy's eyes widened, then teared as she then joined me in uncontrollable cackling.

When I started to regain my composure, I said, "I always wondered what the F.P. stood for," as I began laughing again, this time hitting the floor, rolling.

Amy said, "Stop it!" as I grabbed her and pulled her to the floor tickling her.

"Enough!" she yelled, trying to breathe.

"I'm going to make you stop reading that diary if you don't stop it. It's just not healthy," Amy said giggling.

"Laughter's the best medicine."

"If that's so, why do my ribs hurt so bad. Okay, let me see what else it has to say. Awww...she writes about their wedding and honeymoon. Wow! It was extravagant and all paid for by F.P." she said snickering again."

"Well, that explains why they did what they did for us in Charleston."

"Yes, that was wonderful," Amy reflected and then said with a sigh, "It seems that he had inherited a small fortune from his father. Holy shit, Batman! It says here that he flew them and your dad to their new home in Meadow Lake, Saskatchewan where he paid for their car, home, and some personal items. He seems to have really gotten attached to your grandparents."

"Oh, this is funny," I said. "It tells a story about them going out to eat, and Dad ordered some chili cheese fries. They brought him a block of cheddar cheese on frozen fries. How funny is that, eh?"

"Let me see, what is this? Your grandmother makes friends with a bear who later saves Mark's life. You have some strange ancestors."

"I know, Dad told me about that, and it looks like it's going to be round two with Tony."

"Yeah, but at least he listens, so far," said Amy.

Amy continued, "The diary goes on to say that Nan and Big Guy got jobs teaching on the reserve. Your dad finished high school on his own and went to the University of Toronto. It was there he met your mom," said Amy. "It was also during this time that your dad came up with the idea for Wifi television and F.P. invested the venture capital to start the business."

"I knew that part."

"Oh my God. Well, I bet you didn't know this part. It seems that there was some kind of monster attacking the people of the nearby reserve. Evidently, Master Bennie and his sister Amyra came and talked to your grandparents about the evil spirit that was coming and told them that it was their mission to capture it. I can't even believe this, and yet it's right here."

"Damn, no one will ever believe this either," I said. "A monster called a Wintigo preys upon the town. It kills and devours several people on the reserve. Most think it is a wolf, but as you can read, that is not the case. And it seems only Big Guy and Nan are going to be able to stop it."

Amy said, "Let me see that."

"What does it say?" I said, growing impatient.

"It goes on to say that Big Guy drove his SUV into the school and then went to Nan's classroom to rescue her and the children with a crystal dagger that they both held as they impaled the monster. The evil spirit was trapped in the dagger, and Nan entered a portal and took it to the northern glaciers where she buried it."

Not knowing whether to laugh or cry, I just said, "Unfirkinbelievable."

Amy just leaned over to hug me and said, "I wonder what mission is in store for Tony and whoever his twin turns out to be?"

THE REST of the diary was about my birth, their move back down here to New Bern, my coming to live with them and meeting a girl named Amy, that Nan was sure would end up being my wife. She was psychic after all. It also told of F.P.'s death and his overwhelming generosity by willing the bulk of his estate to my grandparents, them setting up a foundation and some of the charities that they bequeathed.

Toward the spring, Gabriel came by to talk to me about Big Guy's manuscript.

"I finally finished reading through the papers you gave me of your grandfather's *memoirs*. I found it to be fascinating, although unbelievable. Your grandfather had quite an imagination."

"That he did."

"Well, anyway, I think it would make a great novel, but purely as a work of fiction."

"Of course."

"Did you ever finish with your grandmother's diary."

"As a matter of fact, I did."

"I'd like to see it to fill in some of the gaps in the story the old man told."

"Sure, let me get it for you."

Handing him the diary, I said, "You know, I think my grandmother might have had an even greater imagination than Mark. I think you'll see what I mean when you read it."

Laughing, Gabriel said, "I look forward to it. If you don't mind, after I finish looking at it, I'd like to hand this over to a talented ghostwriter that I have on staff. His name is Spencer Michaels, and he has a knack for getting a great cohesive story out of pieces like this."

"I don't mind at all. Whatever you think Gabriel."

NEXT STOP, Disney World! The kids had just gotten out of school for the summer and were so excited to be heading to the airport for their first plane ride. I'll have to admit that I was a little excited myself. This would be my first visit to the Magic Kingdom, too.

We flew into the airport in Orlando and were greeted by the Magic Express, which carried us and all our bags to the hotel. We had booked accommodations at the Polynesian Villas.

"Oh, my! These rooms are exquisite," exclaimed Amy.

"Yes, and look at all the themed murals on the walls," said Seneca.

"Oh yeah, and the comfortable beds," I said plopping down.

"Don't get too comfortable He-Man," said Amy, "we still have two hungry kids to feed after we get unpacked."

"We won't have to worry too much about that," said Gabriel. "We choose a meal plan with dining in the evening, and quick serve meals the rest of the time so that we can eat and go."

"Probably a good idea with two kids who want to see and do and not eat," said Amy.

"Then it's probably also good that the rooms are spacious enough to house two bathrooms so everyone can get up running," said Gabriel.

"Did you know that we have a private swimming pool on our balcony?" asked Seneca.

"You kidding me? Man, this is great!" I said.

The next day we were off and running. Thank God for the Fast Passes that allowed us to avoid the long waiting lines for rides. Combined with the Magic Wrist Bands, navigating the park was a breeze.

We had lunch with Mickey and Minnie and all of the Disney Characters which provided a fun time for all. Then, we hit the rides. First, the teacups, then the Ferris Wheel and Tilt-a-Whirl. We had two daredevil seven-year-olds that wanted to ride Magic Mountain, but I decided to take on the role of the bad guy and said, "No, absolutely not."

"Killjoy pussy fart!" Amy retorted.

And there I was, mouth open, waiting for the flies to land. However, Gabriel and Seneca were relieved, after they picked themselves off the pavement from laughing, so I offered a safe alternative.

"Let's go on the Merry-Go-Round."

"Yay!" everybody yelled.

We hopped on our respective steeds and off we went, around in a circle while the carnival music filled the air with favorite Disney tunes. This had to be the second happiest place on earth. (If you had been paying attention you would already know where the happiest place is!)

We came to a stop, and it was time for everyone to dismount. Tony got off, but a lady, a rather large lady, got off of her horse on the wrong side, consuming my son's head with her fat arse.

Before I could react, I heard Tony yell, "No!" as he propelled the humongous heifer through the air where she landed on Dumbo the flying elephant.

"Fitting," I said.

Amy said, "Er...ice cream?"

"Yay!" said everyone, except Dumbo.

"That boy of yours sure is strong," said Gabriel.

"I'm sure it was just the traumatic experience and an adrenalin rush. At least no one got hurt."

We finished our last night having a Luau at the Polynesian. The feast was incredible and included all of the traditional favorites. We had lomilomi salmon, chicken long rice, kalua pork and all the poi you could eat. Then, everyone learned to do the Hula. The kids were a riot to watch. But watching my beautiful wife Amy really turned me on. Every move was more sensual than the one before. I told her on the way home that maybe she could show me how to do the Horny. As expected, I got punched, and then I went back to the room...and slept on the couch...it was comfortable, too, eh.

Chapter Twelve

*S*ummers come, and summers go. Before I knew it, Tony was nine. Every year, as Tony grew, he seemed to gain a new strength, awareness or ability that we weren't quite prepared for. One such day, in particular, a Saturday, I watched as he went outside to play with his slingshot. (Yes, kids still play with them; didn't you?) But Tony did something else that I was not accustomed to seeing. He was always such a compassionate kid. But that day, he drew back on his slingshot and let one rip right at a bird! The little bird fell from the sky and landed at his feet. I stormed angrily out of the house to discipline Tony, but before I could open my mouth, he reached down and picked up the bird, rubbed it and threw it up into the air. As he did, it began to fly away.

I stood there looking down at Tony, angry and yet so confused. Again, before I could speak, Tony said, "Don't worry Dad, the bird always lives again. Just like Jesus did, I made it fly again. It was easy. It was just made of clay."

"What do you mean, just like Jesus did?"

"I read it in one of your books."

Then, before I could speak further, I remembered having a copy of the *Infancy of Jesus* in my bookcase. I also recalled the story of Jesus making birds out of clay. Fables, oh boy.

"Son, while I know you are curious about a lot of things, you can't use the abilities that you have to endanger a living creature, big or small just to test something you read."

"But it said Jesus did it."

"But you didn't know if you could do it for sure, did you?"

"Well, I know, but it was in a book so it must be true."

"A book, which you can always count on to be true, is the Bible. It says, *You shall not put the Lord, your God to the test.* You could have easily failed in your trial without asking His permission. From now on, ask your mom or me before you try something new out. Sometimes things don't turn out the way you expect, and before you know it, you are in trouble up to your neck."

"Okay Dad, I will," said Tony with his head down knowing he had disappointed his father.

"Why don't you go get the gloves, and we'll play some catch before lunch."

Beaming, he said, "Alright Dad, be right back."

I had watched plenty of reruns of *Leave It To Beaver* when I was a child. I had always hoped that one day when I had children, I could instruct them as Ward Clever did. The one thing I do know is I'm not Ward, and Tony is certainly not the Beaver, and the episodes of this show will last way more than a half-hour.

We were still very tight with the Sparks family, spending a lot of leisure time with them. It had been almost two years since Gabriel had asked Spencer Michaels to start writing Mark's novel. It was probably an arduous task, sorting through old notes and diary entries to come up with one cohesive story.

Then, one day, I got a call from Gabriel. He said that Spencer wanted to meet with me. He had finally finished a draft and wanted my opinion.

I said, "Fine," and set up an appointment.

I'll have to admit that I was getting a little excited at the prospect of actually having this book published, even if they were going to treat it as fiction. To anyone else, it would probably seem that way. But, as I have now learned, fact is stranger than fiction.

Gabriel met me when I arrived at the publishing company. We then proceeded to the meeting room. There sat two other gentlemen whose rose when I came in.

"Sonny, this is Spencer Michaels," as both men extended their hands.

Shaking their hands, I said, "Pleased to meet you both. Which of you is Spencer?"

"That would be me," said a young man in his late twenties.

"And you would be?" I asked.

"Michael," said the older gentleman, around 60, wearing a ruffled polo shirt and khakis.

"Now, I'm confused," I said.

Laughing, Gabriel said, "Most people are. Spencer Michaels is the pen name for a father and son writing team. Michael is the Dad, obviously and Spencer, his son."

"Well, who is the S?" I said, acting a tad like one.

Pointing at each other, they said, "He is."

"Well, again," I said, laughing, "I'm pleased to meet you both. So, where are we?"

Spencer started, "Dad and I have talked about some possibilities with the novel, and we have decided that it should be two novels."

"Two?"

"Yes," said Michael, "The first, would be based on the manuscript that your grandfather wrote through his time in New Orleans, inserting entries from your grandmother's diary to fill in the gaps in the story. We choose to end the book by jumping from New Orleans to your grandfather's last couple of days at Bayview, and him dying on the dunes in Atlantic Beach. Here take a look at the Epilogue and see what you think."

For the next few minutes, I read through the draft and tears filled my eyes. I could barely utter a word after reading the conclusion.

With a few more steps, the sands all fell away beneath their feet, the ocean swallowed itself, and all things physical dissolved—all mortal illusions were revealed and dispelled.

All that was left was one self, and an infinity of stars paling in comparison.

"...Then one by one, the stars would all go out and you and I would simply fly away."

"Guys," I said, choking back the tears, "That is just beautiful. It was absolutely gut-wrenching when I read it, and yet it concluded with a perfect resolution that leaves you satisfied and in a better place. I can only hope that this is how it was for my grandfather."

"We are so glad you liked it. We were thinking about titling the book, *If."*

"Yes, of course, you should," I said smiling, "I think Big Guy would have liked that."

"What do you have in mind for the second book?"

"We are thinking of titling it, *Sopie,* and making your grandmother the protagonist of this novel."

"Sounds like a good idea."

"Well, it's going to be a little different than most sequels as it won't pick up at the end of the story of *If.* It will start with Mark and Sopie leaving New Orleans and ending with Sopie's death in New Bern after they moved back here. It will also cover their life in Canada and their time with F.P.," said Spencer snickering. "Sorry," he said.

"Oh, don't apologize. I was rolling on the floor when I discovered what those initials stood for."

"Us too," said Michael, "Us too."

Spencer continued, "The Canadian sequence will add a darkness to the book that seems to be very popular today. A lot of books written nowadays have become darker and the reader's love it. Look at the *Twilight* series that came out a few decades ago. Those are still in high demand today."

"This ending was a tough one, but I think with the combination of humor, the return of the belligerent Mr. Banos and the hope offered in the final words of the Epilogue, I think we finally nailed it," said Michael, "See if you agree."

Again, I read the last chapter and Epilogue and grinned at Nan's last words, reminisced at how the old man was in the hospital and once again, choked up at the final words,

"And if I go and make ready a place for you, I will come again and take you to be with me, so that where I am, you may be too."

"Of course, she will," Mark whispered tearfully. *Of course, she will…"*

Tears were running down both cheeks, and I just couldn't speak. Then I managed, "As you said, you nailed it. Your writing demonstrates the most beautiful expression of love that I could ever imagine. Thank you."

"No, thank you for allowing us to undertake this project. It has been a lot of fun."

Then Gabriel said, "Sonny, I want you to take these copies home and read through them very carefully to make sure you agree with everything the way it is laid out. After all, it is your story."

"It may be my story, but these guys are the artists who captured the image and painted a beautiful tapestry. If you two do not object, I would like your name to appear as the author of the books, not mine. And I would like you to receive the royalties from the sales. I don't need the money. All I did was supply the story material. I will read through both of the manuscripts in their entirety, but I am positive that I will find everything to my liking. Thank you again, gentlemen, for caring enough about the story to produce this kind of result. I am deeply indebted to you."

As I drove home with the manuscripts in hand, I couldn't wait to share them with Amy. She just will not believe how the books turned out and yet, I wonder what kind of reaction she will have to them.

Amy's reaction to the manuscripts was just as I had expected. She was so moved by the rollercoaster ride of emotions presented, the humor, the sadness that was at times agonizing, the paranormal forces and the overwhelming sense of peace and hope at the conclusion of both stories.

While still drying her tears, she said, "Master Bennie is an absolute hoot. So serious, so sincere, so loving, yet infinitely mischievous."

"Kinda like God?"

"Well, yes. I wish I could have met him when we were in Canada."

"Something tells me that someday you will."

Chapter Thirteen

$\mathcal{T}$he books were released on November 19th of that year and became an immediate success. There were precisely 72,000 copies of each book sold during the first month of their release, and sales just gained momentum from there. It was a beautiful tribute to my grandfather. I wished he could have seen how it turned out. Well, maybe he did. After all, he was only a dimension away.

Gabriel, of course, had read both books, but Seneca, busy taking care of two 10-year-olds, hers and ours, had only had time to read the first book, *If*.

Jodi and Tony both took up Tae Kwon Do, and both became very good at it. I warned Tony not to use his powers to impress, but after all, he was 10. One day his sensei pulled me aside to have a chat.

"Tony is an incredibly talented kid, and he listens well and is always respectful to me."

"Well, that's good to hear," I said, "I was afraid he had done something wrong."

"Oh no, he hasn't done anything wrong. I was just wondering how he could move so fast. When I am working with him on his sparring techniques, it seems as if he just disappears and then shows up behind me."

"Oh really. Well, Tony has always been the fast one. Must have gotten it from his great-grandfather. I hear he was pretty fast too."

Tony tested for his black belt when he turned 12, a remarkable feat in and of itself. He had to break three boards with both a hand technique and a kicking technique as well as an aerial technique. He aced his forms and then there was the sparring. Sensei would not let him spar with the other students as his techniques were too strong. He chose to fight with Tony instead for the test. It started off pretty straightforward, and then Sensei went flying into the wall, appearing to have been struck, but Tony just stood there motionless in a stance.

Then he moved toward Sensei and said, "Oh, I am so sorry. Are you okay Sensei?"

"I'm fine," as the Sensei staggered to his feet, "I just didn't see that coming."

"I apologize. I must have forgotten myself and lost control," Tony said, hanging his head in shame.

"No, it was great, son," said the Sensei, "You have nothing to be sorry for, Il Dan."

"Il Dan! You mean I passed?" Tony said as he excitedly bowed to his instructor.

Tony ran over to Amy and me and hugged us both and then bowed to Jodi, who in turn bowed to him, and then she gave him a big hug and a kiss on the cheek.

On the ride home I asked, "Okay Tony, would you mind telling me just what you did to Sensei at the test today?"

"I just tried that technique that Master Bennie showed Grandpa Big Guy in the book. I didn't know it would work so well."

"It only works for some. And it comes with great responsibility. I told you once before that you might want to check with me before trying something new. We will talk more about it later. Right now, ice cream?"

"Yay!"

JODI SOON ACHIEVED her black belt as well. She was equally accomplished in martial arts even though she didn't have Tony's special hidden talents.

The kids, who were now becoming teenagers started to grow in other areas. Music became a vital part of both of their lives. Tony took an interest in the piano and began taking lessons at age ten. Jodi, believe it or not, had taken up the drums about the same time. Both worked very hard on their music lessons and became pretty accomplished musicians over the next three years.

They started practicing together, forming a little duo called The Dabbs (Jeez). Both seemed very enthusiastic about playing old jazz tunes, and they loved to rock it out with the blues. Tony used one of those keyboards that could mimic about any instrument sound, so when they played, it sounded like a full combo.

"Dad, we were just asked if we could perform at the Morehead City Seafood Festival in May. Would it be okay?"

"Sounds great to me. I'll check with Gabriel and Seneca and make sure they agree."

With Jodi, having just turned 14, I figured it might be wise to check with Jodi's parents, as there was going to be beer served at the event.

Seneca said, "I don't see a problem with it. God knows there is enough alcohol served in our two houses."

"True dat."

"Oh Sonny, I finally got around to start reading your second book. Imagine it taking me almost four years to get around to it," she said chuckling. "I loved the first one, but there always seemed like something got in the way every time I picked the second one up. Oh well, I'm in it through four chapters; no stopping me now," she laughed.

"I hope you enjoy it as much. That Spencer Michaels is quite a writer. I am so glad Gabriel choose those guys to take on the project. Hopefully, everyone made a little pocket jingle."

"I think more than a little," said Seneca.

"Maybe so," I said, "But it is nice to see a piece of your family come alive again, even if it is just fiction. Well, thanks for agreeing to let Jodi play with Tony. The kids are terrific, and they love their music."

"They sure do. I am so happy that Jodi and Tony have developed into such good friends, and I am glad that we have become such good friends as well."

"Me too, Seneca. Goodbye."

The kids practiced hard over the next couple of months before the festival. They were so excited to be playing their first gig. I wonder if this is how Big Guy must've felt when he performed, especially on that night when he invited Nan to see his show for the first time. I somehow think that the two of them must have been encapsulated in their own little world that special night, even though there were hundreds of others in the club.

Breaking through the reverie of my thoughts, I heard my phone ringing. It was Seneca.

"Hello," I said.

"Hi Sonny, I'm afraid I've got some bad news. I can't let Jodi play at the festival. Somethings come up."

"Oh, I hope no one's ill."

"No, just something I have to sort through. Tell Tony that we are sorry."

"I will. Goodbye."

Just them Amy walked into the room.

"Who was that dear?"

"Ah...it was Seneca telling me that Jodi wouldn't be able to play at the festival with Tony."

"Oh, that's really a shame. The kids have worked so hard practicing. Is something the matter?"

"No, she just said there was something that she needed to sort through."

"I'll try giving her a call tomorrow to see if there is something I can do," said Amy. "This is going to break Tony's heart."

THE NEXT DAY Amy gave Seneca a call, but all she got was a voice message that said the number was out of service.

"That's odd," said Amy.

Amy picked up Tony from school that day as she was off for the rest of the week. He got in the car very quietly with a blank stare on his face.

"Hi Honey, have a good day?"

"Not particularly," is all he said.

"Now what's wrong with my little P-Dabb?"

"Stop it, Mom! Please don't call me that again, not ever. I don't want to talk about it."

"Okay," said Amy as she drove in silence the rest of the way home.

Tony got out of the car and immediately headed to his room and shut the door. There was no noise, no music coming from the place, just an eerie silence.

Amy went to the door about a half-hour later to check on him.

She inquired, "Are you okay?"

"I'm fine Mom. I just need to be alone and think."

"Alright, I'm here if you need me."

And she went downstairs to start dinner, waiting for me to get home. It was just not like Tony to ever sulk. All Amy could think about was what in the world had happened at school today?

I finally arrived home.

"Hi, Hon, what's cooking?"

"Nothing good, I'm afraid. Tony is in his room, just laying there looking at the ceiling."

"What's going on? He's not one to sit around and mope."

"I don't know. He won't talk about it. It must have been something that happened at school today."

"I can't imagine what. Let me go see if he will talk to me."

I climbed the stairs and headed for Tony's room. The door was now ajar.

Knocking, I asked, "May I come in?"

"If you want."

"What's going on son? I have never seen you like this. Did something happen today at school?"

"Yeah Dad," said Tony, "something terrible."

"Go on."

"Well, Jodi came up to me and told me that she could not have any more contact with me. She said her mom told her that I was different and she didn't want Jodi to be around me any more than she had to. She said it was to keep her out of danger, although her mom wouldn't explain what she meant by that," Tony said with tears rolling. "I just don't understand Dad, I just don't understand."

Taken aback, I said, "I'm not sure that I understand either. I am going over to the Sparks' tonight and see if I can extinguish whatever problem they have with us before this festers. You haven't done anything out of the way with Jodi, have your son?"

"No Dad, I would never touch Jodi. We have been friends our whole lives. I love her but like a sister. I couldn't...I just couldn't...I would protect her with my very life," he said as the tears came again.

"Okay, Tony. I believe you. Let me see what I can do to help this situation."

Going back downstairs, I told Amy what Tony had said.

"Oh no, I know he's heartbroken. First the festival and now this."

"I think I should go over to the Sparks' tonight and see if there is something I can do to help. Do you want to come along?"

"Yes, I think that would be a good idea."

WE KNOCKED on Gabriel and Seneca's door around 7:30 that evening. Gabriel answered and said, "Come in," although he wasn't his usual jovial self.

Seneca soon joined us in the living room. It was very awkward, so I started.

"We came over to see if there was something that we had done to upset y'all. Tony has been in his room all afternoon, and well, I just don't know what to say. If there is something we have done to offend you in any way, please forgive us. We have been friends far too long now for whatever this is to come between us."

Seneca answered tearfully, "I am afraid it is my doing. I will try to explain what happened and why I feel this way. A long time ago, as a little girl, I was raised by the Flying Dust Cree Nation in Meadow Lake, Saskatchewan in Canada. Growing up, my grand-parents told us many tales of folklore and the Wintigo, as described in your second book. The stories were mainly used, I believed, to scare us children into behaving. However, after reading your book, the tale of the Wintigo was exactly as told by my grandmother. She told me of a man and a woman, who had taught at the school, who were not from Meadow Lake. They had extraordinary powers, and the woman was called Atayohkan by the old chief, just as your grandmother was named in the story. It means spirit being. The carnage they brought on our town was exactly as it was described in your book. The man ran his car into the school, and they killed the Wintigo in the classroom in front of the children. They went away to another place, never to be heard from again. Then, Gabriel tells me that the story came from your grandmother's diary. I was shaking. Surely, this could not be the same Banos' that left Canada. But then I remembered Tony lifting that woman off his head at Disney World and how he sparred with the Sensei at the school and knocked him into the wall without moving. I'm afraid it was much too much for me. I don't want Jodi to be involved in the danger that seems to surround your family. I don't want her to get hurt...or worse."

"But my grandparents saved your village from the Wintigo. They certainly have done nothing but good down here. Have Amy or I caused you to fear us? Has Tony? He loves Jodi, and I'm pretty sure she feels the same way that Tony does right now. Can't we put these old superstitions aside and get back to the way things used to be?"

"I don't know that I will ever be able to release my grief. Sky Roma, the first victim of the Wintigo, was my great-grandmother. I am afraid. They said there was a great evil spirit that took over the Wintigo. It was told that Atayohkan carried a crystal dagger to the glaciers to imprison the evil one. What if he returns? Your family seems to attract death and destruction. How will I protect my Jodi?" she said now visibly shaking.

"I understand. Can we talk some other time again?"

"Yes, just not right now," as Seneca got up to leave the room.

"Gabriel, I'm sorry. I had no idea."

"Me neither," said Gabriel, "Let's allow this to settle down for a while and maybe we can talk again later."

"Okay. Goodnight."

"Goodnight Sonny. Goodnight Amy."

As we drove away, I turned to Amy and said, "I think it's time to have that talk with Tony about the things that Master Bennie explained to me."

"WAS THAT THE BANOS' who were just here?" asked Jodi, coming downstairs with tears in her eyes and anger in her heart.

"Yes," said Gabriel, "they just left."

"I was upstairs and overheard what was said. Is this the way you and Mom are going to leave this. Tony is my dearest friend, and I just can't bear not to see him. Why are you all doing this to me?"

Seneca entered the room and said, "It's for your protection. These Banos' have a long history of danger surrounding them, and I can't stand the thought of seeing you hurt...or worse."

"But Mama, Tony is no danger to me."

"It's not Tony; it's the danger that surrounds his family."

"What do you mean danger?"

"I'm tired of talking about this. Go to your room, and you will just not associate with Tony, and that's final!"

"But…"

"No buts! Go upstairs!"

Crying uncontrollably now, Jodi runs back upstairs.

"Don't you think that was a little harsh?" said Gabriel.

"She's fourteen. She will do as I say."

Gabriel looked down at his shoes, unable to think of anything to say that would make his wife waiver.

In the meantime, Jodi had decided that she just had to get away for a while; to get somewhere where she could breathe and think again. She climbed out of her bedroom window and jumped into the oak tree that was just outside her window. As she climbed down into the yard, she felt two hands support her as she touched down on the ground.

Startled, she heard a whisper, "Hello, little one. Where are you going?"

"Who are you?"

"Jodi, my name is Amyra, and we have much to talk about."

"But who are you, and how do you know my name?" said Jodi a little apprehensively.

"I told you, my name is Amyra. I know much, you not so much. Come, walk with me."

As Amyra and Jodi walked, Jodi could sense that this was someone she had come in contact with before.

"I held you when you first arrived here," Amyra started, "You were at the orphanage at St. Paul's for just a short time before your mom and dad adopted you."

"I was adopted? Who were my birth parents?"

"You didn't have any?"

"What do you mean? You just don't know who they are?"

"No, I mean you literally didn't have any."

"Wait, I know I am only fourteen, but you can't trick me. Everyone has parents."

"Not you. You are different."

"Different? What do you mean, different?"

"You are a divine being, sent here to perform a special assignment...to usher in the twins."

"What do you mean, a divine being? And what twins?"

"You are a divine being, sent directly from heaven."

"Like Jesus?"

"The same. The twins, of which I speak, will be sent here to guide Tony and his twin."

"Wait, I don't understand."

"Don't try to understand now. Just understand that you are here for a purpose. It will all be revealed to you when it is time. For right now, you just need to grow up like anybody else and stick as close to Tony as your parents allow. Don't disobey them. They will come around when the time is right. Everything will be revealed to them when they need to know."

"This is quite a bit for me to comprehend."

"It was quite a bit for Mary to comprehend back in her day, but she obeyed and because she did...well, you see how that turned out. Just listen to your heart and hear God's voice. You will know what to do. Now, let's get you back up that tree and into your room before your parents discover that you are missing."

"Okay, thanks, Amyra. How do I contact you if I need to talk to you again?"

"Don't worry. I will always be there when you need me."

Chapter Fourteen

*W*hen we arrived home from the Sparks' home, the sky had taken on a peculiar hue. The clouds were ominous and swirled above us becoming distinctly funnel-shaped.

As the winds picked up, I yelled, "Oh my God, Amy, it's a tornado."

But before I hardly got the words out of my mouth, the cloud funnel turned on its side, and its vortex revealed a portal before us.

A calm voice said, "Walk closer."

Trembling, we did as we were commanded and found ourselves inside the portal where two younger versions of familiarity met us.

"Big Guy? Nan?" I said, as Amy, with her mouth gaping, just stood there.

"It is us. We thought it was time to give you some additional help with Tony."

"Johnny on the spot I would say."

The young, old man grinned and said, "Unfortunately, revealing some things can cause you problems, as you now realize. However, no real damage has been done. Your friends will recover from their epiphany and move on. More importantly, it's now time to reveal to Tony just who he is and the journey that he is about to embark upon."

Nan began, "The first leg of his journey involves him discovering who he is and what his abilities are. He will need to use these tools soon as it is now time for his full development."

Big Guy continued, "The second leg involves him finding his twin and reuniting with her."

"She may come to him, out of the blue. But he will know without a shadow of a doubt that it is her."

"Who is she, Jodi?" asked Amy.

"Oh no, she is way too much just like him, but Tony will become a crucial ally in completing her divine mission. His twin, however, will be his exact opposite and she will give him a necklace like the one that Big Guy gave me. But don't worry, he will find her when the time is right."

"The third leg of the journey is the trial, and it is very dangerous. It is part of their divine mission here. The twins, upon reuniting, will emit a very high frequency which will add to the healing of this planet. If not for this, the planet would surely die. But Jodi's mission is also vital and I am afraid will be a continuation of the mission that we had while living."

"What do you mean?" I asked.

"We trapped an evil spirit in a crystal dagger decades ago, but with the current climate changes that are going on, there may come a time when the dagger reappears and if damaged will allow the evil spirit to escape and wreak havoc once again," said Nan.

"What will we do then?" asked Amy, "We don't know anything about spiritual warfare."

"Love is the answer. Love conquers all," said Nan, "Faith, hope, and love are all you need. But the greatest of these is love."

"Yes, unlike Master Bennie and Amyra, who helped us, we will not return to help Tony and his twin until much later, so you two will have to help them the best you can with this."

"Great," I said.

"Exactly what I said to Master Bennie," said Mark grinning.

"First, you must help Tony become all that he can be. He must meditate daily to listen to his inner voice. Once he learns to become one with the universe, he will discover all of the abilities that he needs to complete his mission in life. He needs to continue to practice his martial art training to keep his body in shape. He will need to be physically strong to endure the things to come. Unlike me, however, he doesn't need to calm his ego. He has inter-dimensional ability already and is not a showboat even at four-teen...very commendable. Allow him to explore his self, make his mistakes and make the necessary adjustments. It looks like he is going to be an accomplished musician...better than I was. I was always too busy chasing skirts."

And Nan punched him, of course, she did.

"Master Bennie showed up at my dad's funeral."

"He has a way of showing up when he is needed, and some-times when he is not. Don't worry, if you need him, he will appear out of nowhere."

"I don't know how," continued Nan, "but Tony's twin will also appear from nowhere, and no matter what, they will overcome whatever is in front of them, even if it takes them a lifetime as it did us."

"This trial will come after they reunite. They will be ready for it, but I fear someone will have to choose to take the evil spirit to the lower fourth dimension to make sure it cannot return once and for all. The transporter may not be able to return either. The final outcome will only be revealed when it happens. Everything is not predestined. They can also choose not to do the mission as they do have free will," said Big Guy.

"This is a whole lot for a kid to understand. It's a whole lot for us to understand," said Amy.

"Don't worry, Tony will understand. He has understood since he was born. This was his chosen journey. It is up to you two to help him fulfill it."

"We will do our best."

"I know you will. It is time for us to go. We will see you again soon. By the way, thanks for getting my book out. Not too shabby," Mark said, sounding a bit like Adam Sandler as he began to fade from view. "And don't you dare add ice to that single malt..."

And we walked out of the portal to where we began in front of our house. Heaven's gate had closed and disappeared once more. They were gone again.

"Well, looks like it's time to talk to Tony," I said.

"Maybe not tonight. Let him take a day off from school tomorrow, and we'll try our best to explain all of this to him when he's fresh," said Amy.

"Good idea. I'm exhausted from all of this. Let's tell him goodnight and that we will talk to him in the morning. I love you."

"I love you, too."

THE NEXT MORNING was a play hooky day for all. It started with Nan's special chicken and waffles with Crystals, of course, a family tradition. After clean up, we all sat down to discuss the real severity of what was about to happen over the next decade.

"Tony, we decided to spend the day with you today to try and help explain some of the things that are going on with you and some things that are going to happen to you in the near future," I said.

"What are you guys, psychic?" said Tony chuckling.

"Well, not in the way you're thinking, but we'll get to that. This information is going to be a lot for a fourteen-year-old to absorb, but with the recent problems with the Sparks' we felt it was time to reveal to you who you are and why you are here."

"What do you mean, who I am and why I am here?"

"Look, you read both books that I wrote didn't you?"

"Well, yeah, but what does that have to do with anything?"

"Well, they are not exactly works of fiction. The events in the books were pulled from stories your great-grandfather, Mark, told me when he was in the nursing home and from your great-grand-mother's diary. The events in the books are very real."

"Excuse me Mom, but HOLY SHIT!"

"Yeah, I know. But this is why the Sparks' are having problems with us now. It seems that when Seneca was a little girl living in Canada, she was told the story about the Wintigo in great detail, including the names of the people involved. When she recently read the second book that had that story in it, old superstitions started to fester and, to be honest, she is just afraid."

"Afraid of what? Us?"

"Yes, I'm sorry to say. Your Mom and I tried to go over to their home last night to smooth things over but to no avail. The wound is too fresh. Maybe, when this dies down a little, and she realizes that we are the same people we have always been, she will come back around, but not right now."

"Well, what does all of this have to do with me?"

"A little while before you were born, my dad and mom came down to visit us. Dad had been talking to Nan and…"

"Whoa...hold the phone. Wasn't Nan already dead by then?"

"Yes, I can see this is going to take a while to explain. Just bear with me. Anyway, Dad spoke to Nan, and she told him that you were going to be born with abilities, some of which you already recognize, that would emulate Mark. You would have the ability to travel inter-dimensionally and possess the many unique strengths that Master Bennie taught your great grandfather. You remember how you accidentally used that chi force to hit your instructor when you sparred?"

"Yes, I still feel bad about that."

"Well, that's one reason that we are having this talk today. There are things that you need to do to be able to control your abilities. The biggest thing you have to control is your ego. That is a hard thing for most to overcome, but I will say that that does not seem to be one of your problems. Before Dad died, he and I went through one of the portals, liked described in the second book, and talked with Nan and Big Guy to prove to me that these things do exist, so that I could better raise you in the way you should go."

"So, you're telling me that anytime you want to see your grandparents, you just open up a portal and poof, they're there?"

"Not exactly. I haven't seen or spoken to them since you were born, until last night. Your mom and I arrived home, and before we got to the house, a portal appeared. We were then told to come inside. As we did, Nan and Big Guy were standing there and began to tell us the information that I am now going to share with you today. You might want to get your iPad and pencil to jot some of this down as I am sure you are going to want to review this in the years to come."

While Tony went to retrieve the tablet, Amy said, "I hope this is not too much for him. It's a lot for me to absorb."

Returning, Tony said, "Okay Dad, I'm listening."

"Okay, Big Guy said that first and foremost, you must continue to be in tip-top physical shape. Your body will not be able to handle the stresses of what you are going to encounter if you don't get into shape. First, you must meditate daily, to clear your mind so that you can concentrate and focus on what's before you at will. Your inner voice will instruct you as to what you will need to accomplish these things. You need to read the notes for book one and follow Master Bennie's teachings and reflect deeply. These are your new studies. Continue with your music as I know that is your passion, but these studies take precedence over all else. You must learn to cleanse your chakras and develop your chi powers as well as control your inter-dimensional abilities. I know up until now that I have told you to more or less put a lid on it, but now it is time to take the lid off."

"You make it sound like I am some kind of superhuman coming to save the universe," said Tony.

"Well," said Amy, "you actually are one-half of a superhuman coming to save the universe. Which brings me to explain the second thing that will happen. You will meet your other half, your twin."

"Twin? I have a twin?" asked Tony.

"Well, not in the normal sense. You are one half of a Twin Flame, a soul that was divided at birth to experience things on this earth separately. It is now time, or soon will be time, for you to reunite with your twin, which will be of great benefit to the planet."

"How will I recognize her?"

"You will absolutely know her when you meet her. You won't be able to stay away from her once you meet her. She will be the exact opposite of you, a mirror of yourself."

"So, it's not Jodi."

"No, Honey. She is almost a carbon copy of you. Your twin will be different, much different."

"And she will probably give you something that looks like this," said Sonny, holding up Sopie's necklace.

"Is that the necklace that Tom gave Anna in the book?"

"The same. Big Guy left it for me with instructions to give to my first born grandson."

"Okay, now this is getting to be a little much. I'm fourteen, I'm getting married to my twin sister, and we are going to have a son. Jeez!"

Laughing, Amy said, "Not your twin sister, and not tomorrow."

"When then?"

"We don't know. Just take this information so you will be ready when the time comes."

"You will also have a mission to carry out once the two of you have reunited, but I think you have enough to think on for now," I said, "Let's go out and get some ice cream."

"We just ate breakfast," said Amy.

"Soft serve, then."

Chapter Fifteen

$\mathcal{G}$lobal warming was beginning to take its toll with the rising tides in Carolina. Low tides were replaced by what were once the high tides, and the new high tides backed up to most of the buildings and hotels on Atlantic Beach. A sea wall was installed about six years ago to prevent the erosion from the sea. The sea oats were no longer keeping the island intact, and there was now a bridge connecting Emerald Isle with Atlantic Beach in Pine Knoll Shores, where the Old Ramada Inn used to be. I say used to be, as it succumbed about five years ago to Hurricane Margery when the storm cut the island in half, right where the resort had been. Sad times for the Banos family. Lots of memories gone with the tides.

We had now lived more than one-half of the first century of the millennium, and things had changed, and not necessarily for the better. We now were sitting on the edge of our seat, waiting for the new iPhone 55 to appear. Soon, I feel they will implant these things in our foreheads, much like they did credit cards a few years ago. Cars, now all electric, have driven themselves for years now. Funny, it began with a company called Tesla back in 2016. I wonder if they discovered this from one of my real grandfather's plans.

Well, I decided that I should try to teach Tony how to drive the old-fashioned way like Big Guy had shown me. Tony had become very introspective these last couple of years. He did exactly as we had instructed him and enveloped himself in his meditation and martial arts, going deeper and deeper within himself spiritually to absorb every nuance of his abilities, so he would be prepared when the time came. When he wasn't immersed in his spiritual studies, he was practicing his music, perfecting every technique that the keyboard would allow. He became more and more self-absorbed, not that he didn't recognize needs and interests of others, he just wasn't interested.

The family situation with the Sparks', while diffused, did not allow a continued friendship for him with Jodi. Still, they stole time as they could, to encourage each other's dreams and passions. At least, he was smart enough not to take her sailing.

"Come on Tony. I've got something I need to show you."

"What is it, Dad? I'm kinda busy."

"Oh, not that busy, come on."

Tony reluctantly got up from his keyboard and went outside with me.

"What is it?"

"Hop in," I said, starting the car.

"Where to?"

"Cedar Island, or what's left of it."

It had succumbed to the high tides as well. There used to be a ferry service there, but it was no longer needed as Ocracoke Island had vanished beneath the surface two years earlier. Shame, I remember horseback riding down there when I was a teenager, island hopping and racing the horses up and down the shoreline.

"Why are we going there? There is nothing down there anymore."

"I know, that's exactly why we are going. I'll explain after we stop by Uncle Marty's."

I hadn't been by to see Marty in a couple of years. Time flies when you get involved with raising your own family and things like that. I should have stopped by a lot sooner. God, he's got to be well over a hundred by now.

As we drove up, there was Marty in the yard holding a Blue Moon in one hand, as expected, and twirling something in his other.

"Howdy. Come lookin' for these?" he said tossing me the keys to the old S-10.

"Well, yes," I said flabbergasted, "how did you know I wanted to teach Tony to drive...today?"

"Me know much, you not know shit," he said, sounding way too similar to Master Bennie.

"Did you ever meet Master Bennie?"

"Who, the guy that Mark made a cake with? No, never laid eyes on him, why?"

"Just curious. Anyway, yes I would love to borrow your truck long enough to teach Tony to drive the real way."

"Good idea. Just make sure you stay down on these roads. The EPA fines are astronomical."

Laughing I said, "Yeah, I heard."

After leaving Marty, we drove down the old Cedar Island Road.

"Alright Tony, you get behind the wheel, and I'll show you what to do."

"Why are you showing me this? Don't cars drive themselves?"

"Yeah, but it never hurts to learn the old school ways. You never know when you might need to know how to do something yourself."

Tony eased into the driver's seat, a little nervous, something he had not been as of late. He is not used to addressing something outside his comfort zone, another reason I thought it would be a good idea to teach him this. I showed him how to depress the clutch with his left foot, put it in gear and ease it out as he accelerated with the right foot. And the engine cut off with a jump...

"What happened?"

"Got to give it more gas. Crank it and try again."

Tony started it up...and again, THUD, went the engine, cutting off.

"This is not easy."

"Nothing worth learning ever is. Try again."

Starting again, this time Tony pulled out on the road and said, "I did it!" as he proceeded into the ditch.

"Yes, you did. Now get out and push while I try to get us out of the ditch."

After another 20 minutes of quality father and son time, we were ready to go again.

"Now, this time when you get going, understand that you have to steer."

"Steer? We don't have to steer your car."

"Different car, different time. You have to do it all here. No Granddaddy Tesla to help you now."

"Tony, not knowing what I meant, tried again, this time keeping his hands on the wheel, pulled forward."

"I'm doing it!" he cried like he did the first time he rode a bike. And we were off.

Pulling back into Marty's later that day, Tony had a gleam in his eye that I had not seen for a while. This was a good day.

Marty said, "How many ditches did you clear out?"

"Just one," I said.

"Marty, I was wondering...just how old are you now? I know you got to be as old as dirt," I ribbed.

"I planted it, boy," laughed Marty. "Tony, you know you never know when you might need to know how to drive a real truck. They still make them you know."

"As I have found out," said Tony excitedly.

"Sonny, I read the two books you wrote about Mr. B and Anna. They were outstanding, but you know that most of that was just bullshit don't you? I never drank that much."

"Of course I do, it was all bullshit Marty."

"Marty, are you doing alright? Is there anything that you need? I know it's been a while since I got out here to see you."

"I'm fine. You know where to find me if you need me. I am always ready to be of service," he said saluting. "Good to see you, Tony."

"Goodbye Uncle Marty."

"Hey Jodi," yelled Tony down the hall of West Carteret High.

"Hey yourself," Jodi yelled back running up the hall.

"Slow down, young lady," cautioned a monitor.

"Oh, okay. Sorry."

"So what have you been up to all summer. I have barely gotten to see you since school let out."

Tony said, "I've been busy practicing every day, both in Tae Kwon Do and music."

"Yeah, getting your 4th degree by your senior year of high school is pretty sweet," said Jodi admiringly.

Tony said jokingly, "I only wear a black belt because my brown pants are in the cleaners."

"Ah-sole," retorted Jodi laughing and bowing.

"Touché," said Tony.

Jodi said, "Look, I know we have got to keep this on the QT, but can we get together after school sometime? I miss us spending time sharing our dreams and rants like we used to."

"It's okay with me. I would really like for us to get together, as long as we don't get caught. Since we both drive to school now, maybe we can just take a different route home, maybe by way of the marina. What do you say?"

"Yeah, I think that will work. Mom won't miss me as she is helping Dad with some things down at the publishing company and won't be home until after 5:30. Just promise, no sailing."

Laughing Tony said, "That was my dad, not me."

"Alright, I will meet you at the Marina after school."

After school, our Dynamic Duo met down on the pier next to the marina. Dangling their feet off in the cool water, they just sat for a moment and reflected, looking at each other smiling.

"So tell me, Jodi, what have you been up to all summer?"

"Much like you, I have been studying, practicing my drums and Tae Kwon Do. We haven't gone anywhere except down to the beach a few times. Dad has been so busy this year."

"Yeah, we haven't done much either, although Dad did teach me to drive Uncle Marty's old S-10."

"A gas combustion vehicle? How did you get away with that?"

"We went down the Cedar Island Road where no one goes anymore. It was fun driving a vehicle, but it was hard to do. I had to use both feet, steer and shift gears."

"Wow, that is some real old school stuff."

"Man, you can say that again. Given any thought to where you are going to college?"

"I am going to apply to UNC. They have a great music program there."

"No kidding! Me too! They have a great course of study in jazz piano that I have been dying to get into."

"Wow!" said Jodi, "We can see a lot of each other there, and no one will be the wiser."

"Yeah, that would be a great perk. You shouldn't have any trouble being accepted because your grades are off the chart," said Tony laughing.

"Well, I believe yours are maybe a point shy of mine. I think we both have a good chance of being accepted. By the way, I hear you got invited to be the student accompanist for the choral ensemble this year."

"I'm really pumped up about that. It seems to be a great opportunity, and it surely will look good on my resume."

"Well, they are lucky to have you. Look, we had better head back. It's getting late."

"Later, gator!" yelled Tony out of his car window.

"After school, fool!" retorted Jodi as she left him in a cloud of dust.

Chapter Sixteen

"*O*kay people. Have a seat," barked Mr. Finch, the choral arts director. He continued, "This ensemble has six pieces to master in a matter of the ten weeks before the Christmas Fine Arts Evening, so we had best get busy."

The furrowed brow of the pudgy director let you know at once it was time to get down to business. Mr. Finch was a seasoned choral teacher, with fifteen years under his belt. A graduate from Peabody, his abilities were renown. Also, renown was his distaste for sloth. It was something he just did not tolerate.

"Tony, would you take your place at the piano?"

"Yes, sir."

"We'll start with sight singing the six pieces beginning with *I Once Had a Dream* by Purifoy."

They continued to practice for about two hours before Mr. Finch said, "I think that's enough for our first day. I will see you tomorrow afternoon at four o'clock sharp. Don't be late."

Tony was gathering his music to take home and practice when he turned and bumped into the new girl at school.

"Oh, I am so sorry. I didn't see you."

Her broad smile revealed that maybe she was the one that had bumped into Tony, but she said, "No problem. I don't think I'll need an ambulance, maybe just crutches for a few days."

"Really? Are you hurt?"

"No silly, I was just teasing. I'm Myah Matthews."

"Tony, Tony Banos. I have seen you around but never had a chance to bump into you yet."

"Good thing, I guess, otherwise I'd be adorned with bandages," she laughed. "Well, I guess I will see you tomorrow, Mr. Banos."

"I look forward to it, Ms. Matthews."

And as she glided out the door and down the hall, her long red hair just seemed to float in the air behind her. Her hair was not the only thing floating in the air. Tony's world was about to change dramatically.

Choral rehearsals soon became the focal point of each day for Tony, waiting for another opportunity to engage in small talk with Myah.

"So you never told me, where did you live before moving to New Bern?" asked Tony.

"We moved here from New Haven, Connecticut. My dad was an accountant at the hospital in New Haven. He and Mom always yearned to move further south, so when the director of finance position opened up at Carteret General, Dad applied, interviewed and was hired. So here I am."

"Kinda rough I'm sure, meeting new friends in your junior year."

"Oh, I am kinda used to it. Last year, I took a sabbatical from school to study art in Paris. That's why I am eighteen and still a junior. But, I learned to make friends quickly, and as you can see, I already have one."

There was that smile again, coupled with those light brown eyes inside of a ginger complexion. Tony's heart was melting as he hung on to every word she said.

Tony left walking on a cushion of air that day having a superlative spring to his step, right up to the moment he noticed that his car was leaning. He muttered, "Shit!" as he looked at the flat tire that greeted him. He opened the trunk, pulled out the jack and the spare and got to work.

After another half hour, Tony was finally on his way, thinking again about Myah. He imagined being at the beach, tossing a beach ball to Myah and then running to catch her as she sped away. Laughing, holding her, swinging her in the air, slowing as their lips gently met. As his mind drifted, so did his car when Tony reached for the radio and accidentally disengaged the autopilot button. Just then, as he overcorrected the steering, a small dog jumped out in front of him.

"Oh my god!" cried Tony. "I didn't even see it." Jumping out of the car, Tony thought for a moment, looking at the motionless animal that lay on the side of the road. Reaching down, he began to place his hands on the little dog. He closed his eyes, trying to channel his energies to revive the lifeless canine, fully expecting to revive it as he had done before with the birds. Tony, however, was not in the same state of oneness with the universe as he was before. He could not clear his mind and focus on having the creature spring to life. Each time he tried to concentrate, his mind would begin to flood with thoughts of the red haired distraction that had pulled him into this mess. All he could hear was, *"What's the big deal? Why waste your energy on this? It's just a dumb dog. It's over. Think of me. Think of me!"*

The sense of awe and wonderment that had embodied his youth was now replaced with fear and uncertainty, filling his mind with frustration and anger. Despite all of his skills, training and sacrifices, he could not even revive a little dog. How could he complete the *great mission* that lie before him? Tony's thoughts became riddled with doubt. *"What the fuck was I thinking that I would ever be good enough to do that?"*

With his anger now reaching the boiling point, he tossed the carcass in the ditch and yelled, "SHIT!" Even though he felt the warmth of the blood on his hands, he just shrugged with an air of indifference, got back in his car and continued toward home.

But there was a suppressed memory that resounded in Tony's head from reading Mark's memoirs. *"Then my longtime companion, Chivas, died for no apparent reason."*

THE NIGHT of the Christmas Fine Arts Evening was a very formal performance. All of the ensemble, including Tony, were dressed in black tuxedos with seasonal red bow ties. Everyone looked so sophisticated. There was a great round of applause as the ensemble took the stage and Mr. Finch, the podium. After the audience quieted and sat once more, the performance began.

The first three selections went as planned with everyone in the audience giving thunderous applause. The fourth was an a cappella version of *Ave Verum*.

After playing the fifth selection, *Ding-Dong Merrily on High*, Mr. Finch, with brow raised, said, "Tony, pay attention to me for the tempo. That was a little fast."

Tony glared back at the conductor and said, "I think it was perfect, thank you," as he prepared for the sixth and final piece, *Carol of the Bells*.

Tony suddenly copped an attitude that he couldn't shake. *The nerve of old man Finch thinking I was playing too fast. He was conducting too slow. If he thought that was fast, just wait...I'll show him fast!*

And Tony showed him. He played with all his strength and speed as the choral ensemble struggled to keep up. Just as the piece was getting ready to take a sharp right turn into a ravine, Mr. Finch's years of experience and training shined through. He abruptly stopped the music, and slowly brought the chorus in softly and slowly again, a cappella, never breaking a sweat. He ended the piece with a thunderous crescendo in the vocals while slowly echoing the central theme as it faded away. The audience was awestruck and echoed their approval with a standing ovation.

As everyone left the auditorium, Mr. Finch said to Tony, "I

would like to see you in my office tomorrow morning at 9:00 sharp." And he left.

The next morning, Tony impatiently waited for Mr. Finch to arrive in his office. He hadn't given much thought as to his behavior the previous evening as all he had on his mind was seeing Myah later that afternoon.

"Good morning, Mr. Banos," said Mr. Finch.

"Good morning, sir."

"Tony, I wanted to get you insights on last evening's performance, if I could."

"I thought it was fine," said Tony, beginning to show disinterest.

"Fine? That's maybe an overgenerous description from my point of view. I felt the first four selections went well, but the fifth was just too fast, which I know you disagree. But I felt like I was trying to pull the reins back on a horse that was chomping at the bit and fighting me every step of the way."

"Well, I still think it was too slow," yawned Tony.

"That's your opinion, which you are entitled, but not when I am conducting. And what in the world did you think you were doing on the last piece? Showing me who was boss?"

"Well, er...," Tony stammered.

"Or were you just angry because I had to set you straight?"

Tony, now visibly red, jumped up and said, "No, let me set you straight. First, the song was not too fast, second, you are lucky to have someone like me who wants to play for the ensemble, and third, I'm tired of this happy, horse-shit! I will escort myself to the principal's office. Good day."

Then it hit Tony as he walked out the door. *No ensemble meant no seeing Myah every day. Oh my god, what was I thinking? How will I get to talk to her now?*

TONY'S SUSPENSION lasted right up until Christmas break, which would be a win-win for most kids, but not Tony. Throughout the Christmas season, he had no energy. He was just listless throughout the entire holiday. It was as if someone had sucked the life out of him. Amy and I had never seen him so depressed before. It was even worse than the time when he was not allowed to hang around with Jodi anymore. Thankfully, the holidays passed quickly, and Tony went back to school.

Heading to his car, Tony noticed someone following him. Turning around he said, "Well, hey stranger. Where have you been?"

"Oh, I've been around stalking you just waiting for the time to be right to pounce," said Myah.

Laughing nervously, Tony said, "Well, it looks like you got me. Now, what are you going to do with me?"

"Time will tell, time will tell," she said twirling her hair.

"You know there is a basketball game here on Thursday. Would you like to go? Er...support the team and all," Tony said, as he tried to recover from his awkwardness.

"Well, sure. We wouldn't want to let the team down," said Myah coyly. "See ya then," as she turned and walked the other way.

Thursday afternoon the two met and went to the game together. They spent the entire afternoon in idle chit-chat and were still talking when the buzzer sounded that ended the game.

Tony then said, "Hey, would you like to grab a quick bite before we go home?"

After thinking a minute, Myah said, "Maybe next time. I need to get home now."

"Oh, you think there might be a next time?"

"Oh, I'm pretty sure. See ya, Tony Banos."

"See ya," said Tony.

After that game the two became inseparable. Tony walked her to all of her classes and couldn't wait to get out of school so they could cruise around until he had to drop her off at her house. Then he would go through a mini-depression period until he got home just to race upstairs and call Myah on the phone. They spent every weekend together. It was hard to get Tony to do anything around the house, and when he did, it was half-hearted. He couldn't seem to focus on anything other than Myah. When Tony wasn't talking to her on the phone, he was daydreaming about her and then finding an excuse to call her again. He never ate much at supper and took off shortly after that so he could meet up with Myah and continue their never-ending cycle of shit. Everything else soon took a back seat.

Tony then revealed his thoughts to us.

"Mom, Dad, I have something to tell you."

"What is it, son?" I said.

"Well, as I'm sure you have noticed, Myah and I have spent a lot of time together this past year, and well...I am convinced that she is the one. My twin. The connection is way too strong and seems to fit everything, just as you said it would."

"Everything son?" I said. "It seems to me that she is more like Jodi than your complete opposite."

"No, we differ on a lot of things. Like, well, er...she doesn't like to fish."

"Well, there you go!" I said, without thinking, "the perfect opposite. She probably doesn't like scotch either."

"Well, actually, hmmm..." Tony said, deep in reflection.

Amy interjected, "Honey, you may meet lots of girls before you meet THE girl. Don't stress out so much. Just have fun, but be careful."

"Mom, I really believe that this IS the one. I will probably ask her to marry me."

"What about your college plans? What about your music?"

"This is way more important, Mom. It's my destiny."

"We'll see, son," I said. "Just back peddle a little. Give it some time."

"Okay guys, I gotta go. Talk to you later."

Amy and I had mega concerns with this relationship, viewing it as unhealthy. It was almost toxic. Tony's grades at school were sliding…no plummeting. He hadn't practiced the piano in weeks, and his interest in the martial arts was waning considerably. His only thoughts were on Myah.

The senior prom was coming up, and of course, Tony asked Myah to the dance.

"Oh Honey, you both look so cute. Let me get some pictures of y'all before you go. Let's go out back," said Amy.

"Alright Mom, but we have to hurry. We have dinner reservations at Persimmons."

"Well, Mr. Fancy Pants. You are planning a big night! Do you know if Jodi is going?"

"I haven't seen or heard from her in months. I've been kinda busy," he said grinning over at Myah. "Come on let's get this over with. We have to go."

After taking several shots of the couple, I said, "What time do you think you will be home?"

"I probably won't. The prom parties last all night, and we will probably crash at one of those."

"That's probably a better idea than risking a DUI on the highway…or worse. I guess we will see you when we see you."

"Bye Honey. Bye Myah."

"Goodnight Mr. And Mrs. Banos," said Myah as she slipped into the passenger seat.

"Love you guys. See you tomorrow sometime," said Tony, turning to wave and slide behind the wheel. And they were gone.

Tony chose a lovely restaurant. It was the elegant Persimmons Waterfront Restaurant overlooking the Neuse River.

After the maître d' had seated the couple and handed them each a menu, a waiter appeared to take their drink orders.

"What would you like ma'am?"

Myah responded quickly, "Manhattan on the rocks, please."

The waiter, taken aback, said, "Sorry, may I see some identification, please."

"Oh, I was just kidding, water with lemon will be good."

"I will have the same," chimed in Tony.

After the waiter left, Tony asked, "Would you like an appetizer?"

"Yes, I believe I will have the Diver Scallops," she said, choosing the most expensive appetizer on the menu. "I think that mixed with the strawberries, risotto and sunflower sprouts sound very appetizing."

"Hmmm...It does sound good, but I think I will try the fried green tomatoes and pimento cheese on arugula," said Tony. "What are you thinking for an entree?"

Without a moment's hesitation, Myah's eyes moving to the right side of the menu again ordered the most expensive dish. "I would like the prime filet."

"Okay, I'll have the red snapper with clams."

They placed their order and sat back to enjoy the view of the river.

"Oh, thank you, Tony, for bringing me to such a beautiful restaurant. This makes an already special evening so much more special," said Myah, her eyes dancing in the candlelight.

"I just wanted everything to be perfect tonight. For the perfect girl," Tony said with a sigh.

"Oh, that's so sweet. You southern gentlemen sure know how to win a young lady's heart," she said in a faux southern accent smiling sweetly.

After Myah had polished off two desserts, Tony paid the hefty tab for the pleasure of his lady's company and headed to the dance. A good number of Tony's classmates had already arrived, dressed to the hilt in their tuxedos and evening gowns. They had no resemblance to the motley crew that he went to school with daily.

"Well, would you look at you guys. You sure do clean up good," said Tony laughing.

"You don't look too shabby either, Mr. Tony," said George, one of Tony's friends. "And may I say that you, Myah, look stunning. Simply marvelous."

"Well, thank you, George," Myah said in a flirtatious manner.

"Better hold tight of that one, Tony," said George. "She is hot tonight," as he waved his hand as if trying to put the fire out on it.

"I don't need to worry," said Tony laughing, "she only has eyes for me."

As they walked away, Myah looked back over her shoulder to catch George's eye and smile.

They danced the night away...well, I should say Myah danced the night away. She danced every dance with someone, not always Tony. She was having the time of her life and quickly became the life of the party, which ended all too soon for Myah. But then, there were the after prom parties. They went to several after changing into street clothes, drinking a little and a little more at each one. Before whipping into the last driveway, Myah got Tony to pull over for a quick make-out session. Things started to heat up fast, and before Tony knew it, she had unzipped his trousers.

"Do you mind?" Myah asked coyly.

Stammering, Tony said, "I think I'm okay with it." He continued hesitantly, "Are you sure you're okay with it?"

She just grinned as she manipulated his manhood with gentle strokes and then added the moistness of her lips. She slowly flicked her tongue until...he exploded into her willing receptacle.

Myah said with a sultry smile, "Now that was my favorite dessert of the night."

All Tony could do was try to catch his breath. But instead of feeling exhilarated from his first experience, he felt cheap and shallow just as Adam must have from taking that first bite of the apple.

Kissing her on the cheek and then turning away from her in confusion and humiliation, Tony said, "Maybe we had better go in."

Myah said, "Okay, I'm ready to party now," as she checked her makeup and applied a little more lipstick.

They hopped out of the car and went into the last party of the night. Both drank more than enough, Myah to rid any inhibitions that remained, Tony to try to remove any regrets.

The next morning after dropping Myah off at her house, Tony crashed, and I mean crashed. He didn't awaken again until dinner time, and when he did, he had a new experience to share with us.

"Oh, god!" moaned Tony. "My head is splitting."

Laughing I said, "Have a good time last night? Here this might help."

"What is it?" asked Tony.

"Hair of the dog. An old family recipe," I said.

"Smells like scotch."

"It is. Sometimes you have to treat poison with poison."

Tony took a sip and ran to bathroom shouting, "Oh, god! Just let me die."

Just then Amy got back from the store.

"What the hell is wrong with Tony?" she asked as she put her bags on the table.

"Nothing, he just had a good time," I said.

"I see. And what did you do to him?" asked Amy impatiently.

"Me? Just gave him some dog hair."

"And you really thought that would help?"

"It will help...eventually."

Tony reappeared from the bathroom and said, "Hi, Mom. What's for supp..." as he ran back to the bathroom and lost round two.

"He'll be fine. He just has to get it out of his system. I'll bet his head has stopped hurting already."

"Damn stupid Banos thinking," said Amy as she headed to assist her son.

Reaching the door, Tony was just cleaning up.

"It's okay, Mom. I feel much better now."

"Are you sure, Honey?"

"Yeah, I'm fine. I guess the old family recipe works. So what's for dinner? I'm famished."

Tony called Myah later that evening, but her mom answered the phone.

"Hi, Mrs. Matthews. Is Myah there?"

"Actually no, Tony. She has gone out and probably won't be back until late tonight. I think she said she was going to a movie."

"Oh, okay. I'll see her tomorrow. Goodbye."

Tony thought that was odd. *"Why didn't she call and ask me to go with her."*

He tossed through the night, not getting much sleep, wondering what Myah was doing.

The next day at school, he looked for Myah so he could carry her books to class, but she was nowhere to be found. Finally, as he was heading out of the cafeteria, he caught a glimpse of the girl with the red hair.

"Myah!" Tony yelled as he walked briskly down the hall. "Where have you been all day?"

"Me? I've been right here. Why?"

"Well, I didn't see you this morning like I normally do and I missed you. I tried calling you last night, but your mom said you were out."

"Yeah, I decided to go to the movies."

"Why didn't you call me to go with you?"

"Well, to be honest, George asked me to go with him."

"George! What the hell? I thought we had a serious relationship, especially after Saturday night."

"That's just it. I don't want it to get too serious as you are going off to college in a few months and I will be just sitting here by myself, alone. I want to have fun, too. After the prom, I finally got to meet a lot of interesting boys, and I think they are interested in me, too. I really had a great time, but a girl's got to do what a girl's got to do," she said as she glided down the hall to her next class.

Tony just stood there, awestruck. He couldn't believe that the love of his life was going on without him. It was too much for Tony to take. He checked himself out for the rest of the day and went home, to his room, to think. *"How could she do this? How could she say those things?"* The thoughts kept reverberating in his head. Tony got more and more depressed. He laid out of school, his grades dropped further, but he didn't care. All he cared about was Myah. If he couldn't have her, life just wasn't worth living.

He would still call Myah, but she always held to her guns and wouldn't agree to meet him or see him at school.

He started to stalk Myah to see where she was and who she was with. One night he finally caught her with George. The blood boiled through his veins, as he envisioned himself beating George to a pulp. These were emotions that Tony had never experienced. He never had to deal with ego nor jealousy before.

Just as he was about to exact his revenge on the couple, he heard a voice behind him.

"Hello, Tonysan. This is not way to solve problem."

"Who are you?" asked Tony, moving into a fighting stance.

"Shiuh," said the old Asian man.

Recognizing the Korean command to relax, he again asked, "Who are you?"

"I am Master Bennie Hana, mentor to your great-grandfather. We have much to discuss."

"Wait. The Master Bennie? How can that be? You would have to be…"

"Very old," said the master laughing.

"Why are you here?"

"I am always where I am needed. I see you have block that you need some help with."

"Block? I don't understand."

"Not unusual. Dabbs never do. They don't know shit. Me know shit. Now listen and shut mouth."

Tony, mouth hanging open, was quiet.

"Young girl you think is your twin is not, she is false flame, which is bad and good. Bad because you need to rid your chakras of her, but good because she signals in your true twin flame who will arrive very soon."

"I don't believe this. I feel so strongly pulled toward her."

"Aye. But doesn't she take and take from you without giving back anything? Isn't your energy drained? Did you not have a string of bad luck including running over a little dog?"

"Yes, but how did you know..."

"Shut mouth. Told you. Me know much, you not so much. Listen."

Bennie then pulled something from his pocket.

"Here take this. It is a citrine necklace, an old Indian relic."

"That's not very P.C." said Tony.

"And sometime, smart ass is dumb ass. No matter, you not know shit. Shut mouth."

Tony shut his mouth, and Bennie continued, "Hold onto the necklace for two weeks to put positive energy back into your life and get you back on track. Then give it to girl. All of the good will flow through to her, and she will complete her destiny, but no longer be a burden to you. Your life will pass from her, and she will never contact you again."

"But I don't want to be rid of her," whimpered Tony.

Placing his hand upon Tony's shoulder, Master Bennie said, "Have faith in what I tell you. You know it to be true. Trust heart and have faith. There is a much greater joy that awaits you. If she is not false flame, she will not go from you. She doesn't know what she does. It is just her spirit. But you cannot complete your mission with her in your life. You must conquer your past to reach your future. Believe! Love conquers all..." said Bennie as he faded from view. And as he did, a feeling of rejuvenation entered into Tony, filling his spirit once again with unconditional love and thanksgiving.

Totally bewildered, Tony left to return home. Begrudgingly, he did as he was instructed for the next two weeks. His vitality and focus reappeared and the need for seeing Myah waned. Then, one day, came the opportunity to give Myah the necklace.

"Hi ya, Myah."

"Hello Tony," she said turning toward her locker.

"Hey look," said Tony, "I don't want to leave for college on bad terms, so I got you this as kind of a going away present," handing her the necklace.

"Oh, Tony. It's so beautiful. Thank you."

"You're welcome. Have a nice life."

As Tony left her in the hall, he knew that this was going to work as Master Bennie had said as he now looked forward to his new life that lay ahead in college.

Chapter Seventeen

*A*fter re-establishing his GPA, Tony was accepted to my Alma Mater, UNC, as a Bachelor of Music Candidate. He chose this school because it was close to home, offered excellent jazz study courses and...Jodi was also going to attend, pursuing the same course of study. Sweet!

"You know Tony, this campus is a lot bigger than I imagined," said Jodi.

"Yeah, it's good to have at least one person here that I know. Thanks for sticking with me after all the shit I put you through last year."

"You mean the shit you put you through," said Jodi chidingly.

"Yeah, I guess you're right. I did it to myself."

"Ancient history," said Jodi, "Ancient history. I do have someone, though, that I would like you to meet after we get settled. I have a roommate named Ariel, who is an absolute knock out! She's from Kansas and has a very witty sense of humor to go along with a set of *to-die-for* blue eyes and natural red hair."

"Sounds like your trying to set me up with the Little Mermaid."

Tony just couldn't help himself, and Jodi couldn't help herself from punching him.

"I just figured it was about time you got back on the horse," said Jodi. "Besides, it doesn't have to be all that serious. We can just go get some food and drinks, the three of us, and have some fun."

"Okay, sounds great. Just let me know. I think I can work it into my schedule," said Tony, checking the calendar on his phone, which got him punched again.

They decided to go to the Rathskeller in Chapel Hill to get some food and drinks. The restaurant was a remake of the classic Rathskeller of the 1990s. It looked like a place for rats in a cellar as it was semi-subterranean, with small windows providing a tiny amount of daylight. It was very rustic, college and loud. Most nights it was so crowded that you had to literally hang your head out of the window just to change expressions. The menu was the same as when I attended college here. The only thing different was nobody smoked. Anywhere. Imagine that; you could smoke pot in public, but not any tobacco products. They just weren't legal or socially acceptable in public anymore. The place used to be so filled with smoke you couldn't see. Yeah, it used to be great.

Tony met the two ladies there. All three ordered the Double Gambler, which was nothing more than country-style steak and gravy, but delicious. They talked through dinner and seemed to be getting along well.

After a few drinks, six or seven, everybody was feeling their way.

Tony asked Ariel, "Would you like to dance?"

"Yes, very much. Do you mind Jodi?"

"Oh no, of course not. Have fun."

And the magic began with Mr. Wonderful hitting the dance floor. Confident to score big with this chick, Tony put on his best dance moves. He was just twirling her around while doing a Salsa number, totally enamored by his abilities, watching himself in the mirror on the dance floor wall, and then it happened...he saw his reflection looking back at him, but it wasn't him. He caught a glimpse of someone he had not seen, but sensed was there in the room with him. He could smell her smell, feel her touch, without hearing a word he knew her thoughts. She saw him. There was no doubt. She wanted him...now. He immediately stopped dancing and gazed at this woman, in slow motion, her long black hair moving behind her as she waltzed, out of time, out the door. Tony ran for the door, but it was too late. She disappeared into the night.

"What the hell Tony?" said Ariel, as she watched the display. "Go fuck yourself!"

"I'm sorry girls. I've got to go," Tony abruptly said as he threw some cash on the table and left.

Tony went out into the night, but there was no one there. The mental image of the woman of his dreams was embedded in his mind as he frantically and methodically observed the parking lot...but to no avail. She was gone...but somehow he knew, she would be back.

THE COLOR WAS PURPLE. The dress she had worn was purple. Tony groped for details as he combed his memory for every tidbit of information he could recall. She had jet black hair and blue, no they were violet, eyes. She was definitely self-assured. He could tell by her walk. He knew she saw him, but walked away. The game was afoot as Sherlock would say.

Calling Jodi the next day Tony said, "Look, Jodi, I'm sorry that I left so abruptly last night. Please tell Ariel that I apologize as I didn't want her to think I was an asshole, it's just that..."

"It was her, wasn't it?" asked Jodi.

"Yes," Tony said without question. "Now, all I have to do is find this Cinderella who left the ball, but I have no slipper."

"Something tells me you won't need one...and she'll find you. I just know it. This is so cool!"

"And a little eerie, too."

"Well, you Banos boys should be getting used to that by now."

"I suppose. Thanks for inviting me out anyway. Sorry, it didn't work out as we had planned."

"It seems to have worked out exactly as planned," Jodie said as she hung up.

———

THE LEAVES STARTED to green again, and blooms were showing signs of hope from the despair of winter. It was now March, and with March comes March Madness. It was the final game of the ACC tournament, with our Tarheels playing the Blue Devils in Greensboro. Tony was performing with the pep band. He had taken up the bass guitar so he could play with the band during the games. He liked going to the games, and by playing with the group, he had one of the best seats in the house, and the admission was free.

The game had run through the first half, and we were down by six points. Still, we had plenty of time to recover. Tony sat there thinking that he had never seen so much blue. Carolina blue mixed with a dark royal blue all over the stadium. Just a sea of blue. As he watched the crowd, waiting for the second half to begin, he noticed a color that was out of place. It was not royal blue, although close, and it certainly wasn't Carolina Blue. It was...purple. While straining his eyes to get a better look, both teams came roaring back out on the floor as everyone stood and cheered and the lone purple hue disappeared from view.

UNC was now down by two, but Tony didn't care or even seem to notice. It was all he could do to remember he was playing in the band when it came time to do a pep song. Twice the director had to nudge him to keep him on task, and Tony just gave him one of those looks like, *"What?"*

Tony kept smelling the smell of a chili dog. He couldn't get it out of his senses. He could taste it. The aroma was sensuous but...it had slaw on it. Oh God, even though he was officially a Tarheel, he couldn't stand slaw on a hot dog. And then, he could smell the Big Orange soda. *"No!!"* he thought. I can't take this. A Big Orange soda and a chili dog with slaw. It was too much. Then UNC hit a three-pointer as the buzzer sounded. The crowd went wild! And Tony jumped up. And smacked the person with the chili-slaw dog and the Big Orange soda, changing the location of the items from her hands to her...purple dress.

He turned to look in the mirror and said, "I seemed to have developed a sudden fondness for chili dogs with slaw. Care to join me?"

"Yes, of course, I will."

As their appetite for chili dogs had waned, they instead decided to meet at Caffe Driade in Chapel Hill, so the victim of this hit and run had a chance to stop by her apartment and change. Tony sat fidgeting as he sipped on his triple latte macchiato. What if she didn't come back? What if she was really pissed at him? Did his clever remark make him look like an insensitive asshole, and she agreed to meet him so that she could get away?

After waiting another twenty minutes, a black BMW wheels in the parking lot. She flies through the door and immediately gets in line to order her drink.

"I'll have a Constant Comment please," using her phone to pay before Tony could even get up to greet her.

Grabbing her cup from the Barista, she turned to Tony and said, "Hi!"

"Hi," said Tony warmly, "glad you finally decided to join me," covering up his uncertainty that she would.

"Oh, I had decided that a long time ago, but traffic was horrible after the game."

"I'm sure. It took me quite a while to get here myself. By the way, my name is..."

"Wait, let's keep this little mystery going for a while. We have a lot of time to get to know who we are. I'm not going anywhere, you know," giving him the first sign that she knew exactly who he was.

And he was confident that he knew who she was, as he melted from the reflection of himself in her violet eyes.

"So, you from around these parts," using his best Walter Brennan accent.

"No sir, I'm a New York City Kitty," she countered using her Fran Drescher impersonation.

"Oh, I love alien women!" Tony said, sounding just like Robin Williams.

"Silence," she said, putting her hand up and sounding like Dennis Haysbert on the Allstate commercials.

And...Tony was...catching flies.

"You're left-handed. That's interesting," said Tony.

"What's interesting about it?"

"Well, I'm right-handed."

"You have brown eyes. That's interesting," said Violet.

"Yes, I know, because you have violet eyes."

"No, because I can see myself in them."

"Funny, I can see myself in yours. It was one of the first things I noticed about you."

"Oh, you just like seeing yourself, like you did that night at the Rathskeller."

"That WAS you. I knew it!"

"That was me."

"Why did you leave?"

"I was on my way out the door."

"You could have stopped."

"I could have, but you looked like you were busy entertaining yourself."

"I was actually there with a friend and her roommate."

"Then why weren't you entertaining them."

"I thought I was, until...I saw you. You saw me too. I knew it, and I knew you wanted to talk to me. Why didn't you wait? I came out the door as fast as I could."

"Because I didn't know you would be there. I wasn't ready to meet you yet. I knew we'd get another chance."

"And how pray tell, did you know that?"

"Because me know much and you obviously don't know shit!"

Okay, here's Tony...here are flies...any questions?

Not giving quarter, Tony says, "Maybe, I just don't tell people everything I know the first time I meet them. That's all."

"You idiot. I'm not people. It's me, dumbass."

"Oh, I know Violet, I know."

"How did you know my name?"

"Just a lucky guess."

"Bullshit, Tony."

"It's all bullshit."

"Of, course it is. See you later Mr. Banos."

Lifting my cup and rising, Tony said, "I look forward to it, Ms. Westin."

"Jodi!" yelled Tony as he knocked on her door. "Come get a drink with me."

"What the hell? It's 12:30. What is it?"

"I've got something to tell you. Hurry, get your clothes on and come on."

"Oh, alright. Give me a few."

She rushed to throw on some clothes and ran out the door. As she got in the passenger side of the car, she asked, "Have you been drinking?"

"No, not yet, but I am as high as the sky."

"Well, if you have been smoking weed, maybe I better drive."

"No, nothing like that. I'm good, just come on."

Tony pulled into the parking lot on Franklin Street, and the two hiked up to the Top of the Hill Restaurant and Bar. It was one of a few places they knew they could get a drink and talk without yelling. After getting a couple of Red Oaks, they went out on the patio to chat.

"Alright, what is it that's so important that you have to get me up in the middle of the night to tell me about."

"I met her, and we went out and had coffee...well, she had tea and..."

"Wait! Slow down. THE her? How did this happen?"

"Well, as you know, I was at the game. At the end of the game, I spilled her orange soda and chili dog with slaw on her, and she agreed to go out with me."

"Oh shit, I love this girl already. Go on."

"It was one of the most intense meetings I have ever had with anyone. It was like we were sparring. Everything I said she took offense to and then she countered with another remark. It was great. I'm pretty sure the score was tied when she left."

"My God, you are without a doubt one of the strangest human beings on the planet. Did you at least get her phone number?"

"I don't need it. We will bump into each other again, I'm sure."

"Did you at least get her name?"

"Yes, it's Violet. Violet Westin...isn't that just lovely, Violet Westin...Violet," Tony said dreamily.

"Yes, it is just loberly," Jodi jested.

"And she's left-handed."

"She does have two hands, doesn't she?"

"Yes, of course, she does. Why would you ask such a thing."

"Just checking."

"And the most beautiful violet eyes."

"Oh brober, you got it bad."

"Yeah, I got it bad, and it's so good."

"So when do I get to meet the Duchess?"

"As soon as the next ship sails."

"I just want to be sure I approve of the *love of your life*," said Jodi laughing with endearment. "I love you and want you to be happy, always."

"I love you too, Jodi. You have always been my best friend and the only person I could ever talk to about the way my life is. It might seem glamorous for some, but in a way, it's been a living hell, knowing what is going to happen in your life and just plugging along waiting for it to happen. Now another piece of the puzzle has appeared. Thank God, you have been there by my side to help me."

"Of course I am and always will be. Ask me, and I will give it to you. Just knock on the door, and I will always answer."

Jodi continued, "Let's go. I'm tired, and I have an eight o'clock class tomorrow."

TONY DIDN'T *BUMP* into Violet for the rest of the semester. However, he knew she was watching and waiting. Waiting to play the next hand. He may have known how the game was supposed to end, but he wasn't sure how each hand would play out.

Now, you are probably thinking at this point that Tony not only received the gifts that Big Guy had, but had some psychic abilities like Nan as well. Actually no, Violet had the psychic gifts, and she loved to play. Tony had Mark's intuition, but he also had my dad's technological instincts. When Violet came in the coffee shop that day, he quickly took her photo on his handy-dandy iPhone 55 and used the facial recognition app that my dad and F.P. had developed to give him her name. You've got to try to be one step ahead sometimes if you want to stay in the game.Well, as I said, Violet made no contact that semester through the summer.

In the fall, as classes began, Tony had to schedule one religion class for his Gen. Ed. requirements. So, he decided to take a course on the Book of Revelation, as he found that book very intriguing and thought he might as well take something in which he was, at least, interested.

He arrived at the classroom and took a seat. Glancing up, he saw a woman seated in front of him. He immediately recognized her as Violet.

"Well, Ms. Westin, we meet again."

"Oh hi, Mr. Banos," acting like she was unaware of his presence. "And what treat do you have to share with my laundress today?"

"None today, but I can run out and get something if you like," he teased.

"No, just come prepared next time."

Then she stood up and addressed the class.

"Good Morning everyone, I'm Professor Westin."

Chapter Eighteen

*a*s the class ended, Tony approached Violet and said, "Great lecture, Professor. It seems like life is full of little surprises. I had no idea that you were so old."

"Oh, not so old. I finished my Bachelor's in two years as I had dual enrollment in high school. This is my first year as a grad student, and I am an adjunct professor, also my first year."

"Well, you would never know it. Are you a religion major?"

"Oh, no. I have a Bachelor's in English Lit. Let's just say I took quite a few religion courses growing up, so I am pretty well qualified; Catholic School and all."

"When does your last class end?"

"It just did, why?"

"I thought you might like to grab a bite."

"Only if you promise not to spill anything on me."

"Promise," said Tony crossing his heart.

"Alright, Spanky's?"

"Sounds good. I will meet you there."

Spanky's offer traditional college fair, burgers, barbecue and craft beer. The two sat down and looked over the menus.

"What would you like?" asked Tony.

"I think I will have the black bean and barbecue nachos, but hold the barbecue."

Shaking his head, Tony said, "I'll have the Turkey Panini."

The waiter asked, "And to drink?"

"Red Oaks?"

"Fine by me."

Tony started, "So, you're from New York City, went to Catholic School and are a first-year grad school student and professor. And I suppose Westin is from the Westin Hotel Empire."

"Maybe."

"Okay, so why aren't you part of the family business and getting a degree in hospitality?"

"I don't know, why aren't you getting a mathematical engineering degree or at least a business degree so you can run Banos Wifi Communications."

"Well, first of all, I'm a musician."

"Yeah, I could tell by the way you swung that bass guitar around."

"Oh, I just picked up playing the bass so that I could be in the pep band; free tickets and all. I'm really a jazz pianist. I don't want to teach though, just perform."

"Lot of security in that career choice," she said smirking.

"Hey, it's what I do and what I enjoy."

"Sometimes we have to grow up and make choices we don't enjoy so much, like…"

"What?"

"Nothing, I just meant there are more stable choices."

"Well, let me also explain, Banos Wifi was sold a number of years ago when my grandfather discovered he had cancer. My grandmother still lives comfortably in Toronto. My mom and dad make an excellent living at what they each enjoy. He is a statistician with Carteret County, and she is a marine biologist in Morehead in conjunction with UNC. We do okay."

"They do okay. What do you do?"

"I told you, I play the piano. Come see me sometime."

"Music is not really my thing, especially jazz, but maybe I will."

The food and drink arrived, and Tony continued, "So, now that you know the Banos family history, you can answer my question about why your not in the hotel business with your family."

Wiping the dripping cheese from her chin, Violet says, "My family's not in the hotel business."

"But you said…"

"I said maybe."

"Okay, spill. What blows your skirt up?"

"Pardon me?"

"What is your passion, your dreams."

Tony leaned forward, attentively as Violet sipped on her beer easing back.

"I am on track to get a Master's degree in curriculum and instruction so that I can get into administration in the school system. Maybe I will go back and teach at the Catholic School I went to and become principal."

"So, you're going back to New York."

Shaking her head, Violet says, "Oh no, I'm not from New York. I grew up in New Bern just like you."

"Oh, really! Who are your parents? Maybe I know them."

"I don't even know them. I don't know why I'm telling you this, but I was an orphan and raised by a nun. They put me through Catholic School at St. Paul's. I never had anything just given to me. I had to work very hard to get where I am today."

Taking a bite of his panini, Tony reflectively said, "I think that is very admirable and I am sure it was a very tough way to grow up."

"Yeah, it was not so cushy as the life you led," she said taunting. "I had to earn every penny and work through a lot of obstacles."

Leaning in again, Tony said, "Look, just because you are born into money, doesn't make your life cushy. We all have a lot of obstacles before us, and the training to overcome those obstacles has been hard, but I have been relentless. Somehow we will succeed at our mission in life when the time comes."

"What did you say?"

"I said, Just because..."

"No, not that part, you said, our mission in life."

"Yes, and we will succeed no matter what. We have to."

"We?"

"Yes, we dummy. I know who you are and you know who I am, so quit with all of this silliness. You're stuck with me like it or not. We have free will, but we really don't have a choice. We were pre-ordained. So, let's not muck this up. Let's slow down and stop the bantering and the competition long enough to eat and enjoy our lunch. We need time to get to know what there is we like about each other. It seems we already have enough that we don't like," said Tony.

"You're right. I guess there is a lot we need to discuss, but right now let me enjoy lunch with my beautiful new friend," she said finally smiling.

"Jodi, guess who I just had lunch with?"

"Who?"

"Professor Westin."

"Who? Violet? She's a professor."

"Yeah, in my religion class. Then we went out to Spanky's for lunch."

"Cool. How much food did you get on her?"

"None, this time. She sure does like to argue a lot. She puts everything under the microscope. Keeps a guy on his toes. I don't know why she just can't be like you. You and I have been friends since Kindergarten and have had very few harsh words, even when things weren't going so well with my family and yours."

"Yeah, I am glad that finally blew over. I think Mom just came to realize that a person can't be judged by the actions of his ancestors. Although, I personally don't think they did anything bad. They just had a mission, and it saved a lot of lives. Funny how things get turned around somehow."

"Boy, you're telling me. Violet turns everything around. I always feel like I am in a sword fight having to parry the next blow."

"Remember, you two are exact opposites. Don't expect her to like what you like and you probably won't like what she likes."

"You can say that again, slaw on a hot dog and a Big Orange. Jeez. Then, today she orders the black bean and barbecue nachos, hold the barbecue. That's like ordering a pizza with no cheese."

"Have you two had pizza yet?"

"I see where you are going with this. How do you order a pizza without cheese only on one-half. This is going to be tougher than I thought."

"Yes, it going to be a challenge."

"Well, at least we decided to start looking at the things we like about each other and not the things we don't. It may take a while, but I'm willing to try."

"Why?"

"Because it's pre-ordained."

"That's not a good reason. You may have a path, but no one can keep you from going down other paths but you. If you really don't like Violet, don't keep trying."

"It's not that I don't like her, she is just different."

"As she should be. Look, she teaches religion, right?"

"Yeah."

"Well, then go with it. Do your best in her class, and she will admire your attempts to please her."

"Do you really think so?"

"Of course, Silly. If she is into a subject, show your interest at learning from her. She will feel like she is important to you."

"Well, she is beautiful and that body...whoa!"

"Alright, Macho Man. I don't think this lady is going to be impressed with those kinds of remarks."

"Yeah, maybe not. But she is hot."

"Okay, time for you to cool off and start cracking those books before the next class."

TONY STUDIED HARD THAT NIGHT, memorizing the texts and the apologetics within them. The next morning, although exhausted, he felt ready for Professor Westin.

"Good Morning class," began Professor Westin. "This morning I am going to start by reading directly from your text, *Apologetics and the Authority of the Revelation*. If you would turn, please to page 67 in your text."

"IF GOD DOES EXIST, WHY DOES HE PERMIT EVIL?"

After reading from the text, Professor Westin asked, "So what are your thoughts? If God exists, why does HE permit evil?"

Tony's hand shot up. "Tony...?"

"Well, your question infers that evil is a real thing. How do you decide what is good and what is evil? Calling something "evil" assumes that there is a standard of good that transcends the world. That standard of good is God. So your argument against God's existence is not valid."

"So, you are saying that atheists can't tell right from wrong?" asked another classmate.

Tony interjected, "No, what I am saying is just the opposite. Evil wouldn't be evil if there were no God. It would just be things that we don't like. An atheist recognizes evil for what it is. Atheists are like people who can see right away that a dish has been broken, but who can't imagine the potter who created it. What I am trying to say is that these things aren't really evils; it's just stuff we don't like, if there is no God."

"That is a fascinating analogy, Tony," said Professor Westin. "Class we will pick back up on this again in Thursday's class.

Remember to read through chapter eight before you arrive. See you then. Tony, may I see you for a minute before you leave?"

"Sure, Ms. Westin."

"That was a pretty impressive response for a musician," she said chiding.

"Oh, I know a little about the Bible. You knew Satan was the choir director in heaven didn't you?"

"Get the hell out of here."

"Join me?"

"What?"

"For tea?"

"Oh. Sure...five-thirty?"

"Sounds like a plan...see ya."

As they sat in the coffee shop, sipping and chatting, Tony inquired, "Violet, why don't you come with Jodi and me to Jacksonville this Saturday. We are competing in a Tae Kwon Do tournament, and you may get a *kick* out of it?"

"Haha, Mr. Banos. Now, why would I want to go and see you get your ass handed to you?"

"Oh, I don't think there is much danger of that. I'm pretty good."

"Pretty conceded maybe."

"Okay, I just thought you might like to go and see something that I have been involved with my whole life."

"Oh, really I would," said Violet laughing. "I just don't want to see you hurt."

"Well, that's a nice change."

And she punched him as they headed for the door.

"You better do better than that at blocking on Saturday."

Once outside, Tony said, "Oh, you think you can take me? Come on!"

And Tony started tickling her, until Violet said, "Oh my God. I can't breathe. Uncle!"

Saturday came, and the three of them piled into the car and headed for Jacksonville. Poomse (forms) began at 10:00 am, and Kyorugi (sparring) started in the afternoon. Colored belts would be first with the black belt beginning around 4:00 pm. Although neither Jodi nor Tony were participating in form competition, they were asked to be there to judge the lower belt forms.

After the morning's events, they ate lunch (without getting any on Violet) and began to stretch out for the afternoon's competition.

"I must admit," said Violet, "that was interesting watching the forms. Some of those lower belts were extremely good."

"Yes, I agree," said Jodi. "They work so hard on perfecting their techniques. I remember when Tony and I first started. It has been a long road of learning; one that never seems to end."

"It never ends. We just keep getting better and better," ribbed Tony.

Jodi and Tony, again, helped with the judging of colored belt sparring. Then, as it approached four, the two started putting their gear on for the final matches.

The women's competition started with Jodi easily defeating her first opponent, 3-0. Then, two more competitors began. It continued this way for an additional four matches, and then Jodi had to spar another competitor, which again she easily defeated 3-0. It got down to the final two, which was Jodi and this girl from the Virginia Tech Tae Kwon Do collegiate team.

The girl was a fierce competitor, but Jodi gave her no quarter scoring two points in the first minute of the first round. Jodi, then, did a scissors kick, which brought the other girl to the mat as Jodi countered with an ax kick to the head. Jodi was the winner!

"That was fantastic," cheered Violet. "I had no idea that you were able to do the things you did. I am extremely impressed. Congratulations!"

"Thank you," said Jodi, "I was lucky, that's all."

"Lucky you didn't kill anyone," laughed Tony as he prepared for the men's rounds.

In the preliminary rounds, Tony also dominated his opponents. Given his inter-dimensional edge, he easily mystified the other competitors by disappearing and reappearing before their very eyes. It went no better for his opponent in the final match for when he would throw a kick, Tony would counter by disappearing and reappearing behind him striking him in the head with a kick.

"First Place! Banos!" yelled the referee.

"Very impressive Mr. Banos. It seems my fears of you getting hurt were quite unfounded. Congratulations."

"Shucks ma'am, it weren't nothing."

"Thank God, you are not in one of my English classes. Yuck!" said Violet laughing."

The referees gathered in the center of the gym to make an announcement.

"Ladies and Gentlemen. We would like to try something that has not been done before in past competitions. We would like to have a special showdown to determine the Grand Champion. We would like to have the Women's champion and the Men's Champion have a one-point elimination battle for the title of Grand Champion if it is okay with them."

The crowd cheered.

Jodi and Tony just looked at one another, neither uttering a word. In all of the years that they had studied together and worked out, they had never sparred each other. Tony knew he was too strong and might hurt Jodi as this was full contact.

Tony started, "I think this is a bad idea, Jodi." Grabbing the mic, Tony said, "I would like to respectfully decline and forfeit..."

He was stopped abruptly by Jodi, who said, "Not getting out of this that easy, Mr. Banos. I accept the challenge." And the crowd roared.

Tony grinned at Jodi and said, "Okay."

The contest started with both competitors bowing to each other and the referee, who said, "Sijag!" And the match began.

Both Tony and Jodi threw a relentless volley of kicks, ones that would have taken any other competitor that they faced to the mat. Frustration grew in Tony. He had never fought such a fierce opponent as his best friend.

Tony finally used his inter-dimensional bobbing and weaving, which worked great on his unsuspecting adversaries. However, Jodi was different. She had known Tony for most of his life and also knew his strengths and his weaknesses. She could sense his frustration and knew he would resort to using his inter-dimensional abilities. As he started to disappear, she did something very odd. She threw a 540-degree kick, knowing she could stop it at any degree point she needed to once he reappeared and with the added 180 degrees of spin, there would be enough power in it for a point even if he reappeared in the first part of the spin. As expected, Tony reappeared to find her foot at his head, which she mercifully pulled without contact."

"No point!" said the referee.

"No, it was a point! She pulled it so as not to knock me out," said Tony bowing to the referee and then to Jodi. "It is with great respect that I resign...Jodisan."

The crowd went wild. Never before had a competition been decided on love and compassion...not before this one. This was the true Moosado spirit of Tae Kwon Do.

Chapter Nineteen

*I*n late November, Tony was scheduled to perform at his first solo college recital. He had asked Violet to come, but, as usual, she committed in her non-committal fashion.

Violet approached the auditorium with apprehension as she was already late for the recital. Although she was not a huge jazz fan, she was becoming a Banos fan and was eager to hear Tony play for the first time.

The program highlighted his selections:

Tempus Fugit
Dolphin Dance
Bolivar Blues
Someday My Prince Will Come

Tony had just finished *Tempus Fugit* as she slipped in.

"Excuse me," she said as she found her seat.

The next selection was greeted with mixed enthusiasm, as Tony seemed to struggle with the piece. It was as if his mind was preoccupied.

Where was she? Is she coming? He continued to think as he

played mechanically throughout the piece. It was precise, but there was no Tony in it.

As he started to approach the piano for the third selection, he spied a hint of purple in the crowd. She was here! He knew it. He didn't have to see her, he just knew it.

Suddenly the piano erupted as he performed *Bolivar Blues*. The crowd went wild, which was very unusual during such affairs. You could barely hear what was being played. The audience settled again waiting for Tony to finish. When he did, the crowd stood and gave him a standing ovation.

Tony bowed left, right and center as the crowd continued to stand. He went over to the microphone and said, "Ladies and gentlemen, I would like to dedicate this final selection to a very special lady who is here tonight. I won't embarrass her by giving you her name. She knows who she is, exactly who she is, and as I play, I want her to know that I am already here."

The crowd clapped, and Tony resumed his position at the piano and played a remarkable jazz rendition of *Someday My Prince Will Come*.

Tears ran down both of Violet's cheeks. She never cries, but the emotions were way too high on this electrifying night. It was a magical evening.

As he finished, the audience just sat in total silence until there was one clap, then two, as everyone joined in the uproarious applause.

As Tony approached Violet after the concert, she said, "You stinker, you made me cry."

Tony just smiled knowing that he had just won the music industry's highest honor. After all, the only thing any artist wants is for someone other than himself to shed a single tear. The Ice Princess had begun to melt.

WINTER BREAK WAS fast approaching following the recital. Tony had asked Violet to go home with him for the holidays. He noticed that she was fidgeting about on the drive to New Bern.

"Don't look so nervous. My parents are not inspector generals by any means. They will love you."

"Oh, I'm not nervous, it's just that I have never met them and don't know what to expect."

"With my family, you learn not to expect anything, and expect the unexpected."

"I think I have already figured that one out."

As they pulled into the driveway, Amy and I rushed out the door to greet them.

"Hi," we both sang out.

"Hi, Mom," said Tony, hugging Amy. "Hi, Dad," as we embraced. "I'd like you to meet Violet."

"Hi Violet," we both said, "it's so nice to have you here over the holidays. Let us help you guys get your stuff and come on in."

"Hello everybody!" said a familiar voice in the living room.

"Uncle Marty! Merry Christmas!" said Tony, a little shocked.

"We asked Marty to join us for the holidays as he had no one with him this year."

Just then, Angel walked through the kitchen door.

"Dinner will be ready in about an hour."

"Gram! You're here too! This is great. The whole family together, here at Christmas."

"Everyone, I'd like you to meet my friend, Violet Westir."

"Great to meet you," said Marty and Angel.

Once everyone got settled into the living room, Tony asked, "Gram, how long are you going to be down for this time?"

"Oh, I guess nobody told you. I'm down for good. Moved here last month after selling the house in Toronto."

Tony, again sort of shocked, says, "Well, that's great. It was getting too far for you to travel anyway."

"And too cold for these old bones," said Angel laughing.

"Come on outside on the deck, and we will have some drinks. What can I get for you, Violet?" I said.

"Some tea would be nice, thank you."

"Oh, she reminds me of Sopie, my mother-in-law. She always drank tea."

"I'm sure Tony doesn't want tea."

"No Dad, you know better. What do we have for this auspicious occasion?"

"I found an 18-year-old OBAN that I thought you might like to try."

"And I think you might be right."

We all settled on the back porch with the chiminea roaring, rocking in the solace of the early evening.

"Violet," Amy began, "Tony tells me that you are a grad student working on your master's in curriculum and instruction."

"Yes, that's right. I plan on becoming an administrator at a high school someday."

"That's a lofty goal, but I'm sure you will do well."

The doorbell rang, and Amy ran to answer it. There on the doorstep stood Gabriel, Seneca, and Jodi.

"Oh my God. Come in, come in," said Amy ushering in the guests.

"Hey, everybody. Merry Christmas!" said Gabriel taking off his coat.

"Merry Christmas!" echoed everyone.

"I am so glad you decided to come. It just hasn't been Christmas without you," I said embracing Gabriel.

"I know. It has been much too long. We figured with the kids being home from college and all...well, it was very nice for you to invite us to dinner. We just couldn't refuse."

"I am so glad you all came. This makes Christmas complete," said Amy hugging Seneca.

"I've just been an old superstitious fool. I am so..."

"Enough, let's leave the past in the past and celebrate this Christmas as a time of new beginnings," said Amy.

"Come on, Gabriel. Grab a glass and let me pour you some of this OBAN," I said.

"Damn, that was worth the trip. I have meant to try that." Taking a sip of the nectar, Gabriel said, "Oh, my God, that is wonderful. Just taste that toffee. You wouldn't think that four years makes that much difference, but it so clearly defines the notes in the flavor."

We all began to gather around the dinner table as Angel and Amy started dishing out the meal of traditional Christmas turkey and homemade oyster dressing. It was indeed a banquet feast fit for a king.

We then joined hands and began to get ready to ask the blessing.

Tony asked, "Dad, would you mind if I asked the blessing this year?"

"Certainly not. Go ahead, Son."

And then Tony began, "In the name of the Father and the Son and the Holy Spirit,

Jesus' love was unconditional, and it's that unconditional love that brings us together for this Christmas feast with our family and extended family of friends.
Today as we share this holiday meal, may we also share with one another a forgiving and loving heart, as you do for us daily.
May our Christmas dinner be filled with loving kindness. And may the memories of today put aside the bitterness of the past, and give us light and peace for years to come. Amen."

And everyone echoed, "Amen."

"That was so beautiful, Tony. Thank you," said Seneca.

Then everyone began to eat and enjoy a fabulous meal.

After dinner, when the dishes were cleared, and the coffee was served, a rather non-traditional dessert was presented.

Angel said, "Since this is a traditional Banos Christmas, I made a non-traditional dessert in honor of the late Mark Banos. I taught him how to make this once, and...as you may have heard, it didn't go so well when he tried making it himself."

She then unveiled her famous red velvet cake, and everyone began to laugh. It was the biggest hit of the evening.

Marty said, "You know, I had always wanted to try this, but I never had the nerve to ask the old man to make it. Angel, this is delicious."

"Thank you, Marty."

Jodi, who had been unusually quiet this evening, then jumped up and said, "Okay, everyone, let's go in the living room by the tree and sing Christmas carols like we used to when I was little."

"Now, you know I'm not much of a singer," said Tony.

"Well, you can just play, and Violet and I will lead the singing."

"I'm not much of a singer either," said Violet.

"You don't have to be. It's Christmas. Anyone can sing Christmas carols. Let's start with *Joy to the World!*"

And everyone sang along at the tops of their lungs.

Tony said, "I think we may have found a hidden talent in Violet. She has a really nice set of pipes."

"What do you mean by that?" asked Violet, suddenly glaring back at Tony.

"He means you have a nice voice is all," laughed Jodi.

"Oh, okay," said Violet, slightly embarrassed.

"Let's do my favorite," said Angel. *"Silent Night."*

And again they sang with Jodi and Violet leading, while Tony played.

"Oh, I remember my first Banos Christmas with your dad, Sonny. We gathered on the back porch of the cabin. Mark took out his guitar and started to sing that song as it began to snow. Everyone just joined in. It was the best of times...still brings tears to my eyes every time I hear it."

"Yeah," I said, "We have shared some great memories at Christmastime. And now, that our old friends are here again, maybe we can *Sparks* some more."

"Oh, that was bad...phew!" everyone exclaimed.

Rimshot!

Chapter Twenty

*A*s summer approached and classes ended, Tony asked Violet to visit us on the coast. After some reluctance, she said that she would. I say with some reluctance, as Violet discovered early on that her psychic abilities left her with bewilderment as far as Tony was concerned. She had intuitions but never could get a bead on Tony's exact thoughts or intentions. This allowed him the chance for a normal relationship, but it was uncharted territory for Violet. She was not accustomed to uncertainty and did not completely trust someone that she could not discern.

While on the way down to New Bern, she decided she would stop in at St. Paul's and visit with Sister Amyra, as it had been a long time since she was in touch.

"Hello, my child," said Amyra.

"Hi, Sister. How have you been?"

"The same today as yesterday...and tomorrow. How have you been?"

"I'm still working on finishing my Master's at UNC."

"Good. Have you met any interesting people while you have been there?"

"Oh yes, one in particular. He's the reason I have come down to

New Bern. I don't know what to expect with this one though. He is different from anyone else I have ever come in contact with."

"Oh, he is very different. Do you understand why?"

"I think so. I believe he is the one who is my twin. The twin you described to me so long ago, but he is so different from me. We seem to always be in a battle or some sort of competition with each other. And I don't always read him correctly."

"That's because he is exactly the opposite of you. It is like looking into a mirror. Does he know who you are?"

"Very much so. I think I love him and then I think I hate him."

"You don't like people knowing your faults and certainly not pointing them out to you."

"Right! That's it. He is just like looking into a mirror."

"This what makes you two the perfect compliment to each other. As you point out each other's weaknesses, you also build up each other's strengths, making the two of you invincible. You have psychic powers and kinetic powers to overcome your adversaries where he has astral projection abilities to move inter-dimensionally along with physical strengths and abilities. He cannot, however, travel through time and space through the use of portals as you can. Between the two of you, you can overcome anything that is in front of you. However, be cautious, there will be a time when you are with child that you will need to open a portal but do not dare to enter in as it will kill both you and your unborn child."

"Me? I going to have a baby?"

"Oh yes, later. Twins."

"Twins?"

"Yes, very important twins. They will be your mentors for a mission that is yet to come, but that will be much later. Have you had any contact with a girl named Jodi."

"Well, yes. She is Tony's closest friend. At first, I thought she was his girlfriend but found out quickly that she is more of a sister."

"Yes, she was placed here on earth to look after you two until the twins could arrive."

"I'm not sure what you mean."

"You must not disclose what I am about to tell you to anyone. She was here at St. Paul's when you arrived. She, like you, was an orphan. Unlike you, she has no record of parentage.

Shortly after her arrival, she was adopted and raised by Gabriel and Seneca Sparks as their daughter. No one knows any different, and I am sure that's the way they would like it to stay. However, Jodi also has a mission, and that mission is to make certain that you and Tony have a clear path to fulfill your mission."

"And what mission might that be?"

"I do not know yet. It has not been revealed and won't be until the twins come back."

"Come back? What do you mean?"

"Just what I said. They have been returning to earth for thousands of years and just like yourselves, had to fulfill their mission before reuniting their souls and ascending."

"Wait. If they ascended, why are they returning?"

"They now are ascended masters who protect the universe from the evil spirits that might try to escape the earth to enter other dimensions and the evil spirits that might escape the fourth dimension and try to enter earth through an open portal. They will come again to instruct you and your twin as their mentors instructed them until your reunion and ascension."

"This is very confusing. I'm not sure I want to be involved in all of this."

"It is your choice, my child. You have free will."

"It's not that I want to shirk my responsibilities, it's just a lot to wrap my head around."

"I know, my child. Try not to spend too much time analyzing and go with faith. Faith in knowing that all things will happen as they are perfect with the universe's time."

"It's time I gave you this," revealing a small necklace, "It was the only thing you had in your possession when you came here. It is time you took it. You will know what to do with it when it's time."

Looking at the necklace, she saw a gold coin dangling from it, with a face of a man on one side and a woman on the other.

"I'm not sure what this is or what I am supposed to do with it."

"You will, my dear. You will. Have faith."

"Thank you, Amyra. It's been great to see you."

"Go with God, my child. I am always here for you."

WHEN VIOLET ARRIVED, Tony was anxiously standing at the door.

"Hi there. I have been waiting for you. Let's go."

"Go? I just got here."

"We'll get your bags out when we come back. We have a picnic to go to."

"A picnic?"

"Yep! Let's get started."

They hopped in Tony's car and headed East. Crossing the bridge in Beaufort and turning left, they headed toward Cedar Island.

"I have never been out this way before," said Violet.

"New adventures," said Tony mysteriously.

"Just who is having this picnic?"

"We are."

"We are?"

"We are," he said nodding his head. "So sit back and relax."

They drove until the world came to an end. The landscape had changed considerably with the rise in sea level. The old Cedar Island Ferry landing had long disappeared. The ocean appeared miles earlier than it had in years past but was still a breathtaking view. The summer sun was high in the sky, and the sea oats had grown up to protect what was now the new beach area. There were reeds on both sides of the road that kept the beach from view until you were upon it.

Tony stopped and grabbed a blanket and a picnic basket and said, "Come on, we're here."

"Here where?"

"This is where the world begins."

"Or ends," Violet retorted.

"Maybe...I guess it's what you make it."

Spreading out the blanket, Tony opened the basket to reveal a small feast of fried chicken, deviled eggs, potato salad, and pickles, along with a chilled sauvignon blanc. Sitting down on the blanket, the two began to enjoy the wine.

Relaxing her guard, Violet said, "This may be the best place I have ever gone to for a picnic."

"With the best food...homemade not Hormel."

Mellowing Violet said, "And maybe with the best fella, too. Tony, this was really sweet of you. Sometimes you are just amazing," as she leaned over and kissed him on the cheek.

"I know," jeered Tony.

"No, seriously. You put up with my constant bitchiness and sometimes I just don't feel like I have treated you the way that I should."

"Not a constant, and besides, it's probably hard to put up with my ego all of the time."

"Not all of the time," she said as her eyes were beginning to melt.

"Tony started to waver a little, and then began to speak as he pulled something from his pocket, "I was going to save this for dessert, but now seems like the right time."

Opening the small box, Tony said, "Will you marry me, Violet?"

This time it was Violet, waiting for the flies to land as she heard Amyra's voice, "Go in faith, my child, knowing that all things will happen as they are perfect with the universe's time."

She then whispered, "Yes, of course, I will, you dummy," jumping on top of him planting a long deep kiss. "Tony, I have something that I want you to have," unclamping the necklace from around her neck, "This was the only thing I had when I came to the orphanage. Amrya said that I would know what to do with it when the time was right. It is all that I have to give other than myself to you. Please take it."

"I will wear and treasure it always," as they again embraced.

"Hey, Mister," Violet said with tears filling her eyes, "My chicken dinner is getting hot and so am I, so we better eat."

"Probably a good idea. Besides we have an engagement party to go to later."

"A what? Isn't that a little presumptuous?"

"Maybe, but we Banos' try always to be prepared."

"Okay, so where are the utensils for the potato salad?"

"Oops...I said we try..."

WHEN VIOLET and Tony arrived back at the house, the caterers were busily preparing for the engagement party celebration.

"Hi everybody," Tony said dropping off Violet's luggage in the foyer. "I'd like you to meet the future, Mrs.Tony Banos!"

"Well, congratulations to y'all!" Amy and Angel exclaimed. "Let me see the ring."

Violet, beaming, extended her hand to show off the two-carat marquis cut diamond.

"Oh, it's beautiful, and so are you. Welcome to our family!"

"Thank you. Thank you all. You have been so kind to me, and now I hear there is to be an engagement gala. I must admit I am, for maybe the first time, a little intimidated. I am not sure I have something appropriate to wear for such an occasion, and besides that, I don't know anybody. I have been to fancy faculty cocktail parties and dinners, but I was at least acquainted with most of the attendees."

"Well, don't let that bother you in the least. You know the Sparks' and Jodi. They'll, of course, be here. The rest, just think of them as fifty of your closest strangers," I said chuckling. "If you start to feel uneasy, find me, where you will also find some *medicine* to settle your nerves."

"I'm sure," said Amy continuing, "Violet, don't fret, this is just going to be an informal meet and greet; a chance for you to meet some more of our friends in the community. They are not busy-bodies and won't get personal. It's just going to be a floater with the folks helping themselves to the hors-d'oeuvres and cocktails. We're setting up in the dining room and on the back deck so there will be plenty of room for everyone to mingle."

"It sounds wonderful, but I am not sure what I should wear," said Violet.

"Tony, bring Violet's bags upstairs. Violet, let's go see what we can find."

Amy and Violet grabbed some wine and went upstairs, while I went out to the deck with Tony to sample a little bit of the scotches that were to be served. We had to make sure the selections were suitable, of course, we did.

Amy led Violet to her room where there was a zippered bag on the bed.

"Open it," instructed Amy.

Violet slowly unzipped the bag, not knowing what to expect. "Oh my, it is just beautiful," she said as a single tear ran down her cheek.

"I knew you wouldn't know you would need a cocktail dress, so I just picked out something I thought you might like."

"Can I try it on to see if it fits?" Violet asked.

"Of course, you can," laughed Amy.

"Can an old buzzard crash this private party?" said Angel coming up the stairs wine in hand.

"The more, the merrier!" said Amy as she poured herself another glass.

"Oh, Violet, that dress fits you to a T," said Angel. "It was made for you, and you are so beautiful wearing it. Lavender is definitely your color!"

"I feel so eloquent! Like a princess living a fairytale," said Violet, tearing again. "You have made me so happy."

"And you us," said Amy. "Just like this dress, you and Tony were made for each other."

"That I do know," said Violet.

"We had better head back downstairs while we are still able," said Angel emptying the wine bottle.

"Yes, and check on the boys before we have to go back out to restock the scotch," said Amy.

The Sparks were the first of the guests to arrive.

"It is so good to see you again, Violet," said Seneca.

"It is nice to see you again, too, Mrs. Sparks."

"None of that now, I'm Seneca, and this is Gabriel," she said hugging her.

"Hey, Jodi!" Tony yelled, leaving his sanctuary on the back deck.

Hugging him, Jodi said, "Well, you finally did it. I guess this means I can finally get some sleep without someone waking me up in the middle of the night to talk."

"Maybe," said Tony.

Violet punched him.

"Definitely!" Tony said laughing.

For the next three hours, the guests poured into the home to wish the couple a happy life. It wasn't long before Violet allowed herself to become very comfortable in her new surroundings, without the aid of my *medicine*.

As the guests were finally leaving, I noticed something new that Tony was wearing around his neck. I asked, "What is that you are wearing?"

"Oh, this is a necklace that Violet gave me after I asked her to marry me. She said that it was the only possession she had from her childhood."

"May I see it?"

"Sure."

"Tony, would you come with me. I have something to show you."

"Sure Dad," excusing himself to Violet for a minute. "What is it?"

"I'd like you to take a look at this."

Tony gazed at what I held in my hand and said, "You showed this to me a long time ago when you explained what Big Guy and Nan told you. It looks like an exact duplicate of the one I have, except for the crease in it. What exactly are these?"

"It is the sign of the Twin Flames. It proves that Violet is your twin."

"Oh, I already knew that from the beginning. We just had to work through a few things."

As Tony handed me back the necklace, something felt odd.

"What the Hell?" I said as I looked down at the necklace, which now had split into two exact duplicates. "Tony, did you hand me your necklace, too."

"No Dad, I put mine back on."

"Well, would you look at this?" as I showed him the two necklaces that split from the one.

Tony said, "I guess now, this is where it begins to get interesting, eh?"

"Oh, I am afraid so. I am afraid so."

Chapter Twenty-One

*a*fter all the antagonism, competition, bantering and arguing, it turned out that Tony and Violet really did love each other. They, now, had a renewed respect for each other and each's abilities. There's was a love that had to be earned, although unconditional love was never a question. And I'm sure that because of this, it may end up being the greatest.

The wedding was a relatively simple one. It was held at St. Paul's Catholic Church, here in New Bern. Our family was, of course, there but there was no family on Violet's side except Amyra, the nun who had raised her. Uncle Marty made the occasion since I offered to drive him. Jodi stood in as Maid of Honor, and Tony asked me to be his best man. Jodi's parents were also in attendance. Oddly, though, they stayed behind and visited with Amyra instead of attending the reception.

After the sweet ceremony, we all went back to my house, where I had hired a caterer to handle the wedding dinner and reception. We began the meal with a salad of endive, pear, and watercress with a blue cheese vinaigrette. Then we feasted on a rack of lamb with onion-potato au gratin and boiled haricot verts. Côte-Rôtie was the perfect pairing for wine. The French apple tart topped with some sweetened crème fraîche made a nice ending. And of course, the scotch overfloweth.

After dinner, Amy's parents, Billy and Elva and my mom, Angel wanted us to take a ride with them. They said they had a little surprise for the newlyweds.

As we were driving, Billy said, "Oh, I forgot to get something. Can we swing by the marina for a minute and stop by my office?"

"Sure," I said.

As we pulled into the marina, there at the dock was the Karli Anna, refurbished and decorated with white bows and a sign that said Just Married.

Angel started, "We knew you kids were going to wait to go on your honeymoon after the school year, but we figured you might like a place of your own for the night."

Billy said, "This ship brought a lot of joy to your grandparents, not so much for Sonny. I will make sure you two get proper sailing lessons."

Laughing Amy continued, "Just don't let Captain Sonny offer to take you for a ride."

Tony said, "I don't know what to say. Thank you all."

Violet echoed tearfully, "Thank you."

Inspecting the craft, Tony picked up Violet and said, "Welcome aboard Mrs. Banos."

AFTER EVERYONE LEFT, Tony said, "Well, what do you think about being abandoned on a ship with me for the night."

"I don't know, you scurvy knave. You wouldn't try to take advantage of me wouldst thou?"

"Aye. I'm sure I might."

"And what if I refuse."

"Then maybe I will make you walk the plank."

"Then, I guess I have no choice but to give into your desires. Alas."

Tony then picked her up and laid her on the bed covering her with kisses.

As they became more and more passionate, their clothing soon disappeared. Engulfed in their passion, the couple shared love's embrace...

And the world stopped. Their reunion of spirits collided and sent out a frequency that was so high and amplified that the cabin windows shattered upon their release.

The cabin windows were not the only thing that shattered, however. At the top of the world, a crystal dagger that had been carried there many years ago had become unearthed by the melting glaciers. It, too, was affected by the extreme emission of high frequency and shattered, releasing an ominous presence.

"I'm free again. Now to finish what I started."

TONY AWOKE the next morning to the smell of freshly brewed coffee and *bacon!*

"What's cooking?" he groggily said as he looked at his bride sitting in the middle of the floor cooking on a Coleman camp stove.

"Good morning, Sweetheart. I thought I would fix my husband breakfast on the first day of our new adventure together," said Violet.

"Smells wonderful, but do you think it's safe to use an open fire on the deck of a boat?"

"Of course it is, silly. I laid a fire retardant rug underneath the stove."

"Oh, okay. What are we having?"

"Two, two and two."

"What, pray tell, is two, two and two?"

"You really don't get around much. Two eggs, two pieces of bacon and two pieces of toast. Coffee?"

"Yes, please," he said as he gave his bride a squeeze and a kiss on the cheek.

After a few sips of the steamy beverage, he began to regain his bearings...and inspect the damage to the shattered windows of the boat.

"Whew! Looks like the Karli Anna wasn't weather-proofed for a Banos-Westin wedding night."

"Oh, I think it weathered the storm quite nicely," she mused as she sipped on her tea and flipped the eggs with the spatula.

"I guess our first order of business this morning, after breakfast and dessert, is replace the windows."

"You brought dessert?"

"Oh, yeah!"

"Whoa, Cap'n! Aren't you afraid we'll sink her?"

"I'm prepared to go down with the ship," he said as he picked Violet up and swung her around.

"Okay, okay! Enough. Eat first, then dessert, if you are not too full."

"I think I'll have room," Tony said wryly.

Tiding up the cabin after *dessert* the two of them headed to the marine store to get some glass cut for the boat windows. After giving the clerk the dimensions, they waited for him to cut the new pieces.

"We are just going to have to be more careful next time," Tony said.

"Yes, we will just have to be more careful," Violet said giggling.

Handing the newlyweds the glass and some marine caulk, the shopkeeper said, "Y'all be careful out there."

Bursting into laughter, they said, "That's the plan, that's the plan." And out the door the went.

After arriving back on board, they prepared the windows for the new panes. Reinstalling the glass and sealing around the frame with the caulk, Tony stood there admiring his handy work.

"Well, you ready to test them out?"

Laughing, Violet said, "Maybe we ought to give them time to

set. Why don't we head down to Beaufort? I'd kinda like to stroll through some of the old shops."

"Sure, and maybe we can stop and get a Shackelford Shores Sand Bar while we're down there. It's been years since I had one."

They proceeded down Highway 70 East toward the coast. There had been many changes down that way since I was a boy. For one thing, the bridge between Morehead and Beaufort was longer. Longer due to the fact that Radio Island had submerged and succumbed to the sea as the climate changes had dramatically altered the landscape. Tony was too young to remember how there used to be a bridge to the island and then a second one that connected the island and Beaufort. Now it was just one long suspension bridge that hovered high over the sound.

Beaufort was still pretty much intact, although they had to move all of the shops and docks back about three blocks due to the rising waters that eroded Front Street. Cedar Street, which is Highway 70, became the new Front Street and the town rebuilt everything as it used to be, including the docks. Dad always told me to buy all the land I could afford because they weren't making it anymore...well, now they're making less of it.

"Oh, Tony! Look at this bikini and cover-up. It even has sandals to match."

"Imagine that. It's almost like the shop owner said, *Violet's coming in today...Quick pull out the purple clothes!*"

Punching Tony squarely in the arm, Violet said, "Watch it Buster or no dessert tonight! And I thought you liked me in purple," she said, pouting just a little.

"I *love* you in or out of your purple clothes," said Tony coyly.

"Really?" Violet said with a slight smile.

"Really," said Tony.

"Okay...we'll take them!" she said snatching up the garments.

Heading out the door of the shop, Tony said, "Let's go down to Farmer's Coffee Shop and Bakery to get a Shackelford Shores Sand Bar."

"What exactly is a Shackelford Shores Sand Bar?"

"You've never had one? Really? It's a dark chocolate candy bar encrusted with sea salt. Delicious."

"Lead on," said Violet.

Entering the coffee shop was like going into a doughnut shop; too many aromas, too little time.

"Two Shackelford Shores Sand Bars, please," said Tony finally getting the girl's attention from behind the counter.

Not looking up but pointing in the general direction, she said, "They're over there on the other table if we have any left."

Looking on the table, Tony sees the sign and the price. *"Thirty-six dollars! Holy smoke they have really gone up since I was a kid,"* he thought as he gazed below the sign to find the display empty.

"Excuse me," trying again to be granted an audience with the girl behind the counter, "there are no bars left in the display. Do you have any more?"

The counter girl said, "Nope."

"Will you have some later today?"

"Doubt it," she said, cracking her gum.

"When will you get some more in?"

"Whenever the owner gets around to making more...maybe Wednesday or Thursday, but surely by Friday."

"So, if I come back on Friday you will have some then?"

"Doubt it."

"But you just said..."

"I said she would make them by then. They won't be set and wrapped until later."

"When do you suppose that might be?"

"Dunno. No way to tell."

"Thanks for the information."

"Glad to help, now I have to get back to work."

Violet, not believing her ears, just had to jump in, "Doing what, catching flies for Beelzebub? You have got to be the most incompetent employee I have ever seen. You don't greet your customers, or recognize they are even here, and then you are too lazy to help them find what they are looking for. Then you can't even tell them when they can come back and get what they want. AND from the sounds of things, your sloth has been passed down to you from the owner of this establishment. What is your name? I want to report you."

"Oh, it's Francine. I'm the Farmer's daughter. And there they were...mouth's ajar...catching flies. Step back, Tony. No Shackelford Shores Sand Bar for you."

As the two were once again meandering down the sidewalk, they noticed a chill in the air as the wind picked up. Tony and Violet dodged into the Old General Store to peruse the offerings.

"One of these hoodies might be nice on blustery days down here," said Violet.

"Oh, I don't think you'll be needing a hoodie anytime soon, at least not with me steaming around."

Just then, they heard the weather service on the store's short-wave radio.

Small craft advisory is in effect from 3 pm today through 6 am tomorrow. Gail force winds are expected to reach 60 mph. This warning is issued for all of Carteret and Craven counties....

"We might want to head on back. We may have a rough night of it," said Tony.

"Oh, I know I will be safe if I am aboard with Capt. Tony," said Violet lovingly.

"Yeah, somewhat safe."

"Yeah, somewhat," said Violet blushing.

JODI HAD DECIDED to go down to the beach that day as well. She needed to get away to clear her thoughts and gain insight into the trials to come. She decided to take a walk on a now deserted stretch of beach near old Fort Macon. There had once been an education center and a lovely state park beach with concessions, but since the rising of the tides, the remnants of the fort were all that remained.

As she rounded the point, Jodi, deep in meditation, passed a strange looking old man sitting on top of a big flat rock. She glanced and smiled as he said, "Hello there."

"Hi," she said as she smiled again and continued to walk away.

"Nice day for a walk, mind if I join you?"

A little apprehensively, she said, "Well, I guess it would be okay."

As he drew nearer, she noticed his face was like leather, weather-worn from years living near the sea. His teeth, the few that he had, were stained due to heavy tobacco use. His disheveled appearance was crowned with an old fishing cap that had Capt. Stacy Fishing Charters embroidered on it.

As they walked, the pungent odor of sulfur seemed to ooze from the old man every time the breeze would blow. Finally, he said, "I can't help but notice that you seem to be in deep thought. Anything I might be able to help you with?"

"Oh no, it's nothing. Just some things I have to work through."

"Well, you know, you don't always have to work through things; you do have free will. You don't have to do them at all."

"That's not the case here. I just have to prepare myself for what is to come."

"None of us knows what is to come, after all, we're not psychics."

Not saying any more Jodi continues to walk.

"You know, as young as you are, you have your whole life ahead of you. You can have anything you want...anything. Why don't you quit fretting over the things you think you have to do and go and have fun. Get out there and do what you want. Get the things you want to have. Find a nice fellow, settle down and have a kid or two. You could live in a nice home near the ocean and kick back and live the life. Tony and Violet can fend for themselves. You deserve a life, too."

Stopping abruptly in her tracks, Jodi says, "What purpose does it serve to gain everything in life, just to lose your soul. Get behind me, Old Nick!"

As Jodi looked over toward the old man, he was gone. Jodi had finally received the answer that she had sought.

When she returned home, Jodi continued to notice that both her mom and dad displayed an unusual demeanor around the house. They were moping. Jodi couldn't ever remember them ever spending time moping, even when her mom had discovered the truth about the Banos ancestors. Jodi finally decided to ask them about it.

"Mom, Dad, I've noticed that ever since the wedding, you guys have just been really down. Is there something wrong?"

Seneca began to tear up and then said, "We had a long talk with Sister Amyra over at the church after you all went to the reception and I guess it's time we talked to you about it."

"To start with," Gabriel interjected, "we need to tell you a few things. First of all, and understand we never tried to hide anything from you, but you are not our biological daughter. We adopted you from the orphanage at St. Paul's shortly after your birth."

"Guys, I've kinda known that for some time. It's no biggie. One person left me at the church because they loved me and you guys adopted me because...well, you loved me. I don't see a problem."

Seneca said, "That's not the only thing we have to tell you. It seems that you are a divine being on a mission that is to transpire soon. During this mission of yours, we...we," Seneca said as tears are freely flowing, "may lose you."

"Lose me? You'll never lose me. My spirit will always be with you. I have known for some time of the trial that is ahead but believe me, it is what I was born to accomplish. If I do not attempt this trial, then I cannot continue. Please don't weep, but be joyous in my sacrifice. It is the ransom for so many."

"We are trying, honey," said Gabriel, "it is just so very hard."

"I understand, Dad. It is not easy for me either. Maybe, whatever this mission is, I will be able to overcome it and come back to you. But if it is not to be, be glad. Be joyful that I was able to fulfill that which was meant to be. It will be fine, and I will return, I promise. Just keep looking skyward. I love you guys. Say, let's go get some barbecue."

"Big Oak Drive In?" her parents uttered.

Jodi smiled and started singing, "BODI, BODI, BODI, BODI, BO! Oh yeah."

Chapter Twenty-Two

*W*hen the kids arrived back at the boat, Billy, Amy's dad, greeted them saying, "We need to put the *Karli Anna* on the trailer tonight. With this gale coming in, it is too dangerous for you two to stay on the boat tonight. Neither of you has enough experience to weather a storm like this on a boat. Come on. I'll help you get her out of the water."

Tony and Violet followed Billy's instructions and prepared the boat to weather the storm.

I had just pulled in as they were getting ready to pull it onto the trailer.

"Whoa!" Billy said, "I think the kids have got it."

"Never gonna let me live it down are you?"

"Nope," Billy said grinning. "You kids can bunk with Elva and me tonight. That way you won't have to bother with a hotel."

"Or dessert," Tony muttered.

Violet punched him and said, "Thank you so much for your generosity." Glaring back at Tony, Violet continued, "We'd be happy to accept your hospitality."

Grabbing what wasn't tied down, the newlyweds headed for Billy and Elva's.

Hellacious winds and rain surrounded the community that evening. They discovered that the torrential downpour from the night before had created a lake in Billy and Elva's front yard as they began to head back to the marina that morning. There was damage all the way down, everywhere you looked. Shingles missing, siding blown off of houses and mobile homes completely demolished.

Holding their breath as they entered the marina, they just couldn't believe their eyes. The boat slip at the dock, or what was left of it, had been replaced with lumber from the remains of the boat that was housed in the slip next to it.

"Oh my god, if we had stayed here last night we would have been killed," said Violet still in a state of shock.

Tony slowly turned to look at the *Karli Anna* expecting the worse. Their boat, however, was unscathed. It just glistened in the morning sun.

"Time to take lessons from the master," said Tony quietly.

IT WASN'T LONG before Tony and Violet became very proficient in sailing and caring for their sailboat. They spent a lot of time perfecting their sailing techniques on the weekends on the Neuse.

When they weren't sailing with Capt. Billy, they were at our house barbecuing and drinking scotch, of course, they were. We loved spending time with the newlyweds, and they seemed to enjoy our company as well. Amy and Violet became the best of shopping buddies, and Violet soon started calling Amy, Momma B.

Naturally, with both kids finishing college, they still needed to maintain an apartment in Chapel Hill. It wasn't that far from New Bern, and they ventured back down to the coast just about every weekend. They continued to stay on the Karli Anna and use it as their temporary home, but both Amy and I knew that that fantasy life would be short-lived, especially now that Violet was three months pregnant.

"Tony, I think it's time we find a more permanent solution to our living quarters."

"I think I have to agree with you. There is not much room on the boat, certainly not enough to raise children. Why don't we contact a realtor and see what we can find?"

"Me thinks you are a wise man, Tony Banos."

"Let's get dressed and see what's available."

After breakfast, the two called the realty firm that the Banos' had used for years, ever since moving to New Bern. They, then, went to Don Hinkle's office to see what was on the market.

"Hi Don," said Tony. "This is my wife, Violet."

"Hi Tony, Violet. It's nice to meet you. What can I do for you?"

"We are in the market for a home in the New Bern area, preferably somewhere on the Neuse."

"Well, before we get started, let's look at what your needs are. You told me on the phone that you're expecting twins, so school districting may be important to you."

"That's not going to matter in our case as we plan to send them to the Epiphany School of Global Studies. It would be nice, however, to be close to it."

"I understand. Let's take a look at what you want inside the house. How many bedrooms would you want?"

"At least three and preferably four with 2 1/2 baths."

"Okay, and I assume a large living room area and kitchen."

Violet interjected, "Yes, a huge kitchen with granite countertops, and a large dining area. I love to cook and would love to be able to entertain."

"I would like a large den or office area that I can use for a music studio," said Tony.

"And we would love to have a wraparound porch and deck that leads down to the river. We have a sailboat that we would like to dock at our home instead of having to run down to the marina each time we want to use it," continued Violet.

"A good sized yard is also imperative. Plenty of room for the kids to play," Tony said as Violet clasped his arm smiling.

"Okay, sounds like you guys pretty much have in mind the kind of place you are looking for. Anything else?"

"Yes," said Violet, "Purple shutters."

"Purple shutters?" Tony and Don just looked at each other scratching their heads.

"Well, it would be nice," Violet said whimsically.

"Okay you guys, give me until next weekend, and I will search the MLS and private listings to see what we have to meet your desires. It was nice to see you both."

"Nice to see you too," they both said leaving.

"As they approached the car, Tony looked at Violet and said, "Purple shutters...really?"

"What?" as she sashayed to the car door.

THE FOLLOWING WEEKEND, as promised, Don contacted Tony and Violet.

"Hi, this is Don. Can you two meet me at one o'clock? I think I may have found the home you're looking for."

"Sure, where do you want to meet?"

"Just swing by my office, and we'll ride over to the property together."

"Sounds good," said Tony, "We'll see you at one."

After arriving at the realty office, Don drove the two to a riverfront community in Minnesott Beach.

As they pulled into the driveway, Violet exclaimed, "It's got purple shutters and a purple door as well as a purple railing around the wraparound deck! It's beautiful."

The white estate house was a beautiful blend of country elegance and city charm. They went inside to discover four bedrooms, two and a half baths, beautiful hardwood flooring with heated tile in the bathrooms.

"This kitchen is absolutely marvelous. Look at these countertops and the hanging rack for my pots and pans. Is this a wine cooler?...It is! Oh and look at the dining area."

The living room overlooked the back deck, just like the one over at Amy's and my house.

Tony, then, discovered the den.

"Look," he said. "There is enough room in here for my studio and an office."

Closet space was everywhere. No problem with storage.

"Let's go downstairs, guys," said Don, motioning toward the basement.

They climbed down the steps to find that the whole area was finished with an additional half bath.

"Sweet!" said Tony.

"Tony, I already know what you're thinking and NO Man Cave. This will be a playroom for our children."

"Well, it could be a playroom for the adult child as well. It's big enough."

"We'll see," as she noticed Tony's lip protruding in a pout.

Climbing back upstairs, they went out on the back deck and noticed that the deck did, in fact, run down to the dock where the Karli Anna could now reside.

Looking at Tony dreamily, Violet said, "What do you think, Pop?"

"I think I will never hear the end of it if we don't buy this. Get the contracts, Don."

"Got them right here. Let's move to the kitchen where there's a flat surface to write on. What offer do you want to make on the house?"

"What is the asking price?"

"3.4," said Don.

"Is that a fair price?"

"You could offer less and see if the owner will accept it."

"But is the asking price a fair price?"

"Yes, given its location and the square footage, condition of the house and time it has been on the market. The owner has also agreed to do a pest and home inspection and provide a one year guarantee against defects."

"We don't want to try to get him to take less if the house is worth it. We always want to be completely above board and honest in our dealings. We just want to buy the house. We have decided this is what we want. If we will pay him what he asks it will be a done deal, right?"

"That's right, said Don. "Have you received a pre-approval from the bank for the mortgage?"

Laughing, Tony said, "No, I will just right you a check. To whom do I make it payable?"

Violet gasped, and this time it was her, sitting there, mouth open and waiting for flies.

AFTER DON HAD DROPPED the couple off at their car, Tony noticed that Violet, who is usually a gabber, was extremely quiet.

Tony said, "Is there something wrong? Have you decided that maybe that house isn't right for us?"

"Oh no, it's perfect. I was just shocked when you wrote a check for 3.4 million dollars is all."

"Oh that," Tony said smiling. "Well we Banos' have a few bucks stashed away for a rainy day and in case we happen across a superb bottle of scotch."

"Yeah, but I had no idea you had that kind of money."

"WE, you and I, actually have that kind of money, but it's not something I have ever wanted to advertise, and I try to keep it in perspective. I have just been very fortunate, and I try to remind myself of that."

"I am curious, though...how did you come into such a windfall. I know you're grandfather owned a cable company in Canada, but surely he didn't make that much money."

"He and Mark made a small fortune off of that venture. Their partner, F.P. put up the seed money. He was filthy rich, beyond measure, and when he died, he left everything to Big Guy and Nan. They set up a foundation in his name to benefit others with most of the money, but the royalties keep coming in from IKEA, and Dad and Mom set up a trust for me to start receiving a part of that when I turned twenty-one."

"IKEA? What does that have to do with it?"

"That's a long story. To make it short, F.P.'s father created designs for the company's founder and because of that, he and now his heirs receive 10% of the company's profit. I didn't tell you because I wanted you to fall in love with me for my charm and good looks."

"Well, I fell in love with you despite your lack of charm...but you do look mighty fine, Mr. Banos. By the way, what does the F.P. stand for?"

"Don't ask."

"Why? I got to know."

"I am not even going to try to explain why his parents named him this, but his first name was Firkin."

"You're kidding me, right?"

"And for his middle name, he was named after his mother's great uncle...Percy."

"They named him, Firkin Percy and they thought that would be a good idea?"

"It was okay in Denmark, but not so much here in the U.S."

"I'll bet he got his ass beat."

"Not for long. As I understand it, he was a Marine veteran and then worked in the field for the FBI."

Violet, somewhat saddened, said, "You know, I bet he led a lonely life. To think, having all that money and nothing better to do than to give it to the likes of you."

"Yeah, very sad indeed," said Tony laughing, "but in all seriousness, the foundation that Big Guy and Nan set up has done so much good for so many people. I can't begin to tell you of all of the dreams that money has fulfilled."

"Well, it just fulfilled another one...with purple shutters," said Violet, as she leaned back relaxing in quiet meditation.

Chapter Twenty-Three

"Tony, we need to find a church," Violet announced.

"A church? For what? We are already married."

"For the children. It will give them grounding."

"Okay, do you have one in mind?"

"Well, I hear that Pleasant Valley Congregational is a non-denomination church that is very progressive and it is said to have excellent daycare facilities. Pastor Bob is the preacher there and from everything I hear, is a man who really delivers God's word."

Tony, remembering the words of Master Bennie in Mark's memoirs said, "You know, Master Bennie once said that church is sometimes good, sometimes not so good. It has one body, but 200 minds. What's wrong with St. Paul's?"

"Nothing. It's just old and stodgy. I was thinking maybe a more progressive church might be a better match for us."

"Maybe. We'll try it and see."

The next Sunday, Tony and Violet arrived at Pleasant Valley. It was a beautiful modern facility that echoed *Welcome*.

"Seems inviting enough. Let's go in," said Tony.

The service was just about to begin, and of course, the newcomers sat in the very back.

After the praise band began to play some songs, Tony whispered, "This isn't half bad. They don't have music like this at St. Paul's."

"I told you."

Then Pastor Bob came out dressed in jeans, plaid shirt, string tie and a herringbone jacket. He looked a little bit like Elvis did during his puffy, last concert days with no facial hair except for those long, mutton-chop sideburns. He began:

"Good Morning!"

"Good Morning!" everyone responded.

"Before we get started this morning, I wanted to give you an update on Sister Lydia. She has been moved from the hospital room and back to Bayview Nursing Home. She will have to continue with physical therapy there, but seems to be completely out of the woods, so far as recovering from her recent stroke."

"Hallelujah!" said someone in the congregation.

"Great is our God!" said another.

"And a mighty God is He!" shouted Pastor Bob.

"Amen!" echoed several others.

Pastor Bob then said, "Now let us give back a portion of that which God has so richly blessed us."

The congregation then resounded into singing the Doxology:

Praise God, from Whom all blessings flow;
Praise Him, all creatures here below;
Praise Him above, ye heavenly host;
Praise Father, Son, and Holy Ghost.

After they had finished singing, Tony said, "Well, I knew that one."

Violet just glared back at him with her finger to her lips, as Pastor Bob began to deliver his message.

"Friends, we just performed a duty instrumental in keeping God's work alive. By giving your tithes and offerings to this church, you provide for its many ministries. The Bible speaks clearly on the subject of tithing beginning with the first tithe in Genesis 14:20:

And Abram gave Him a tenth of everything.

And in Genesis 28:22 Jacob states:

And of all that you give me, I will give a full tenth to you.

The Bible further states in Numbers 18:21:

To the Levites, I have given every tithe in Israel for an inheritance, in return for their service that they do, their service in the tent of meeting.

In other words friends, the Lord established the tithe as payment to the priests for their service."

Violet was beginning to squirm at this. This was scripture, but not exactly in context.

Bob continued. "In addition, the Bible says in Amos 4:4-5:

Come to Bethel, and transgress; to Gilgal, and multiply transgression; bring your sacrifices every morning, your tithes every three days; offer a sacrifice of thanksgiving of that which is leavened, and proclaim freewill offerings, publish them; for so you love to do, O people of Israel!" declares the Lord God.

This clearly states that the Lord requires more than just the regular tithes. In our case, you should look toward additional giving so that we may build a new multi-purpose building that will allow more outreach to our community and its youth."

"As we leave our doors today, there will be ushers with baskets to receive your additional gifts to begin our building fund."

Then the praise band began its final hymn, *"Everything and Nothing Less."*

After the hymn, Tony and Violet got up and were the first out the door since they were sitting in the last pew.

Pastor Bob extended his hand to Tony saying, "Welcome to our church. I'm Pastor Bob."

"Hi, I'm Tony Banos and this is my wife, Violet."

"Pleased to meet you," returning his attention to Tony, "Seems that you are enlarging your family soon."

"Yes twins, in a couple of months," Tony replied.

"Great! They will love the use of our daycare facilities as well a the new family center when it is built. We are taking up offerings for that now. Would you like to contribute?"

"Not quite yet. This is our first visit and we haven't decided on a church home yet," said Violet. "Besides, I would like to hear a sermon on something other than just giving. Some of the things I heard today seemed to be out of context."

Pastor Bob just grinned patronizingly. He then turned back to Tony saying, "If tithing is not reinforced scripturally, then the church itself will begin to fail. There is a lot of good that we can do for the surrounding community with the multi-purpose building."

"That makes sense to me," said Tony, reaching for his wallet.

"We'll discuss it when we get home," said Violet, heading to the car in a huff.

"Tony, I guess you had better get your wife's permission first," said Bob tauntingly.

"I don't need my wife's permission to do anything," he said, throwing a hundred dollar bill in the plate. "See you next Sunday."

Tony headed to the car and got in. He found a chilly reception and a silent ride on the way home.

Arriving back at the house, Tony said, "I don't understand what you are so mad about. After all, you are the one who said we needed to find a church. Pleasant Valley seemed good to me. What's going on?"

"Didn't you notice the condescending attitude that Pastor Bob had toward me? He only addressed you and spoke to you when I addressed a concern," said Violet.

"No, I really didn't."

"It seems to me that the only thing he concerns himself with is how much money he takes in, twisting the scriptures to make the point he wants to make...and he's a chauvinist," Violet continued.

"Now, I don't think that's quite fair. That's not what I saw at all. I just think he is trying to enlarge the facilities there and needs to make the congregation aware that it takes a lot more than just prayer and good intentions to make it happen," said Tony. As far as him being a chauvinist, I don't even know the man and certainly not well enough to judge him and maybe you shouldn't either. Why don't we just try it again, one more

Sunday, and then decide whether or not this is a good fit for us or not?"

Begrudgingly, Violet agrees. "Maybe I was a little too sensitive to his remarks and you're right, I don't know him well enough to judge him. We'll try it one more time. What could it hurt?"

"WELCOME BACK TO PLEASANT VALLEY," said the greeter shoving a bulletin in Tony's hand.

"Thank you," said Tony.

Violet and Tony looked for the comfort of the back pew once again. Tony smiled at Violet knowing the reservations that she had being there.

Again, the band began the service playing several praise choruses. Once they finished, Pastor Bob approached the pulpit.

"I wanted to share this message with you today, that has been pulling at my heart," continued Pastor Bob.

"Bless your heart," said an elderly lady in the first pew.

"Thank you, Sister. I usually don't deliver the message until later, but today I am being led to share this with you now, before the offertory. It is to be of great importance to your salvation and the continuation of the church itself. Let me begin with scripture as all that is worthy is based on scripture."

"And he said unto them, Take heed what ye hear: with what measure ye mete, it shall be measured to you: and unto you, that hear shall more be given."

"Amen," echoed the congregation.

"For what is a man profited, if he shall gain the whole world, and lose his own soul? Or what shall a man give in exchange for his soul? Soul winning is the dearest thing to the heart of God (Romans 10:15)."

"Hallelujah, Brother," someone shouted.

"In 2nd Samuel 24:25, David presents burnt and peace offerings to the Lord to turn away God's wrath against Israel. God had sent a plague upon Israel which had already killed 70,000 people in just three days. The Lord accepted David's offerings, and then the plague stopped."

"Friends, if you want the pain and suffering to stop, you MUST be willing to sacrifice. Place your faith seed of $5,000 in my church and expect that your faith seed will produce a great harvest."

Violet started to squirm in her seat again, feeling very uncomfortable at these words.

Pastor Bob continued, "You will then see:

That God will use this gift and send the Holy Spirit to your home. I'm asking God to give you a visit from the Holy Spirit, to be your financial advisor who will use his secrets to enhance your life.

That God will use this $5,000 seed to activate every failed crop that did not grow in past years. God will use your obedience today to begin a new life for you in the future. Whatever the Devil stole from you will be returned unto you seven-fold."

"Remember friends, that delayed obedience is disobedience. Delayed obedience to God is certainly a sin."

Not believing what she was hearing, Violet couldn't contain herself any longer. She jumped up and yelled, "LIES!"

And the walls of the church almost caved in as the congregation inhaled.

"Delayed obedience to God is a sin. This is the only thing you have said that is true. You used scripture, but you used it wrong. The Bible speaks about people like you in Matthew 7:15 when Jesus said, *"Watch out for false prophets. They come to you dressed as sheep, but inside they are vicious wolves."* You are twisting scripture for your own gain. If you want to use the Word of God, why don't we look at 2 Timothy 4:3 which clearly says, *"There will come a time when people will not tolerate sound teaching. They will collect teachers who say what they want to hear because they are self-centered."*

You're coming out here telling hardworking people that in order to gain God's favor they have to pay you five thousand dollars! You are quoting Romans which is saying that we are to share the message of salvation, not swindle people with empty TV evangelism. 2 Samuel 24 has nothing to do with "seeds" but repen-

189

tance. If you read verse 10 and 17 of the same chapter, you will see that David's conscience began to bother him, and he confessed he had sinned and asked forgiveness. As always, sacrifice to the Lord is a form of restoration and repentance. In verse 24, David paid 50 pieces of silver for the threshing floor and oxen, even though it was offered to him for free. David said he couldn't offer a burnt offering to God that cost him nothing. He wasn't buying favor from God; he was giving of himself. Let me explain this in simpler terms for you; David wasn't giving God his freebies.

After a long, uncomfortable silence, a long time parishioner rose to speak.

"Little lady, what you say is scripturally correct. I can't believe I have been listening to this wolf in sheep's clothing. I am ashamed for having come to this God-forsaken place," said the old man in the congregation, getting up to leave.

Another man got up with his family and started to leave. Before he did, he said, "As for me and my house, we will follow the Lord."

"Friends…" Pastor Bob started.

"You are no friend of mine, Jesus is my friend, you greedy devil," said a mother leading her children out the door.

To calm things, Bob had the band play a final hymn, *"Blest Be the Tie That Binds."*

Soon after that, the remaining congregation left silently out the door leaving Pastor Bob standing in the vestibule.

Another Pleasant Valley Sunday.

"WHEW!" said Tony. "I don't believe I have ever seen you that riled up before. And I don't think I have ever been more proud of you. You really do know your stuff, Professor."

"What he said was wrong and it just really upset me. I'm sorry I caused such a stir, but I'm sorrier that I asked you to go there with me."

"You couldn't have known what was going to happen. But if you think about it, maybe the universe put you in the right place at the right time. You just may have saved a lot of people thousands of dollars."

"Maybe...but I think I would like to raise my children in stodgy, old St. Paul's."

"HELLO? Yes, this is Pastor Bob. Well, I never intended...that's not what I meant...hmmm...I see. Any chance of you reconsidering? I understand you feeling that way but..." *click* went the phone on the other end. And that's the way it had continued throughout the week.

Call after call from disgruntled members saying they were taking a break or had decided that Pleasant Valley just didn't have the right feel for them spiritually anymore. Some were just out and out rude about it, bordering on threatening the pastor. Oh, there were one or two feeble calls of support from long-standing members who were just too kind to do anything else but share words of encouragement. Then the bell tolled again. This time it was the doorbell. It was Stan Kershaw, chairman of the board of deacons.

"Why hello, Stan," said the weary pastor, "Come in and have a seat."

"Hi Bob, Thanks."

"Would you care for a drink? I just made a pitcher of sweet tea."

"No thanks, I won't keep you long."

"So what's up?" asked Bob nervously.

"Well, after the commotion and accusations at the service Sunday, I, as well as other members of the board of deacons and the board of trustees, received numerous calls from upset members asking for your removal from the pulpit. This afternoon, both bodies met and deliberated for some time. We unanimously decided that the best solution for all involved was to ask that you resign your position."

"And if don't?"

"You will be voted out at the next business meeting."

"That hardly seems fair after all that I have done to make this church what it is today."

"Bob, I didn't want to have to bring this up, but what happened during the service is not the only point of concern that we were faced with in making our decision. It seems that there has been quite a bit of discrepancy in the amount of the offerings and the actual bank deposits each week. In addition to that, we discovered that the reason Miss Carrington left the congregation a year ago and moved away was not due to an ailing mother. Congratulations Bob, it's a boy."

Visibly shaken by these revelations, Bob stammered, "You'll have my resignation in the morning."

"Thanks, Bob. You know it's the right thing to do," said Stan as he stood and headed out the door.

"WHO WAS THAT WOMAN?" thought Pastor Bob as he sat at the table that night in his home, deep in thought. He was preparing to eat his last supper as he sipped on the last bit of wine. He figured suicide was the only avenue left for him.

Angrily, he thought, *"I have worked so hard over these last five years, to build that church...now it's gone, all gone. How will I be able to pay my bills now? Damn busybody, Miss Smarty Scripture Pants. Where the hell did she come from? I'd like to kill her and take her to hell with me. Then I'd have my revenge..."*

"REVENGE IS MINE SAITH THE LORD..."

"What the hell? Who said that?"

"Who do you think it is?"

"God, is it you?" Bob said shakily.

"I am who you say I am, so I must be."

"What do you want with me, your willing servant?"

"REVENGE."

"But how? And why do you seek me to help you?"

"I know whom I can trust to do my will."

"Okay," he said shakily, "what do I need to do."

"Receive the bread before you, and I will come upon you."

As Pastor Bob took the bread, he realized that this was not the Lord, but he didn't care. He, too, wanted revenge and the evil spirit entered into him saying, "What we do, we must do quickly."

TONY AND VIOLET entered their apartment in Chapel Hill after spending another weekend in New Bern. Tony had just one more week of classes before finals.

The couple started to settle in on the coach when Tony said, "Honey, I know you have to be tired from the trip. Tonight, I will fix dinner and you just take your shoes off and watch a little TV."

"Awww, that's so sweet. Thank you," sighed Violet.

Violet began channel surfing when she stopped on a TV evangelist show. There, presenting the message, was none other than Pastor Bob.

"Tony, come quick!"

"In a second, I'm mixing my omelet."

The pastor began, "Vengeance is mine saith the Lord. I am the Lord's hands, Violet!"

"Tony!"

"What?"

"Look, it's Pastor Bob!"

"Our Pastor Bob? Where?"

"Right there..." pointing in the direction of the TV.

Looking closely at the set, Tony said, "I don't think Gordon Ramsey looks anything like Pastor Bob."

Violet stared at the screen seeing a rerun of *Kitchen Nightmares*. She said, "I must have changed the channel. I swear to you it was

Pastor Bob and he said, "Vengeance is mine saith the Lord. I am the Lord's hands, Violet."

"He said, Violet...specifically called you by name. I think maybe you are just overtired from the trip and dozed off."

"Maybe you're right. But it seemed so real."

Tony said, "If you are going to be alright, I'm going back to finishing the omelet before we have a kitchen nightmare."

"Sure, I'm fine."

After a delicious dinner of omelet, asparagus, and English muffins, Tony cleaned up while Violet got ready for bed. Tony soon joined her as they tried to get some rest for the next day.

"I hope I can sleep. That episode this afternoon was so vivid. It's hard to believe it was just my imagination."

Tony said, "Well, tonight's dreams will be nothing but sweet. Goodnight."

THE ALARM SOUNDED bright and early at 7:45 the next morning. Unfortunately, Tony's first class was at 8:30. Grabbing a doughnut and heading out the door, he left Violet on her own at the apartment as she had no classes left to teach this semester.

Arriving on campus at 8:25, Tony realized that he left his briefcase filled with his final compositions for class. He quickly texted Violet to see if she could bring them to him. She agreed, grabbed the case and headed for campus. So much for a leisurely second cup of coffee.

She spotted a pacing Tony on the street corner, parked, got out and handed him the music.

He, in turn, kissed her on the cheek and raced to class.

Violet then decided that since she was already on campus that she might as well have that second cup at Aromas, the campus coffee shop. It was a nice day, so she walked the block to the coffee shop.

She opened the door to be greeted by a vast array of aromas, hence the name Aromas. Freshly brewed coffees, fresh pastries, and scones.

It was too much for a pregnant woman to endure.

"I'll have a Breve, no Latte, no Salted Caramel Mocha and a cheese danish and a blueberry scone and a Mars Bar!" said Violet, drooling over her choices.

After finishing her breakfast buffet, she decided to head back toward home. As she got nearer to her car she noticed a man speaking, standing on top of a wooden box. It was an all too familiar sight of a street corner preacher on campus. But as she got closer, it became all too clear that this was not an ordinary preacher. It was Pastor Bob!

"Repent! Repent saith the Lord. Your day of reckoning is drawing close, Violet. Hear my words. Those twins will never be born!"

Violet turned to run to her car but tripped on a speed bump in the pavement. She fell face down on the ground. Violet tried to get up but she could not.

A nearby student, seeing what had happened, rushed to her side and said, "Don't move. I've already called 911."

When the EMTs arrived, they took Violet's vitals and decided to go ahead and move her to the hospital. Tony, who had been called from class, arrived at the North Carolina Memorial shortly thereafter.

"Violet Banos," Tony shouted at the admissions desk, "Where is she?"

"She's in with the doctor in the ER. Are you her husband?"

"Yes."

"You can go on back and fill out the admission forms later."

Flying through the ER, "Tony greets Violet and the doctor."

"Honey, I was so worried. What happened? Are you alright?"

"I think so. The doctor just said that all I have are scrapes and bruises."

"And the twins?"

"I did an ultrasound and checked the babies' vitals. They are doing fine. No cause for alarm," said the doctor.

"What the hell happened?"

Violet said, "I was leaving the coffee shop when I saw Pastor Bob preaching on the street corner. It startled me when he said, "Repent! Repent saith the Lord. Your day of reckoning is drawing close, Violet. Hear my words. Those twins will never be born!"

"Hearing that voice...calling out my name...I started to run, caught my foot on something, tripped and fell. The next thing I knew I was here."

"Honey...Pastor Bob again? I saw that street preacher on my way to class. I'm sorry, but it was just Frank Markley. The same guy that has been there all year."

The doctor interjected, "It is not unusual to have delusions just before the end of a pregnancy. Violet is obviously worried about the health of her babies. But let me assure you both that there is nothing to worry about. The babies are fine. Sometimes the mind just plays tricks on us and if these thoughts are allowed to fester, they seem to become manifested in everyday settings. Daily meditation, to calm your mind, would be a great start, but I think the best prescription in your case is to go back to your home on modified bed rest until the twins are born.

"I think you are right, Doc. The stress of expecting twins coupled with driving back and forth each week, while I finish my degree, has been too much for her," said Tony.

"But what about your final exams? They're next week," said Violet.

"You let me worry about that, Honey. I can arrange to take the exams online. That way I can stay home with you. It's time we head back to New Bern and wait for the birth of our children."

Chapter Twenty-Four

"Oh shit!"

"What is it, Honey?"

"I think contractions are starting."

"Oh shit! I'll get the car."

"Wait. It's okay, there going awaaaay...Oh...SHIT!"

"I'll get the car. Where are the keys?"

"They're in your hand...oh shit!"

Tony had methodically planned this trip, packing the suitcase, preparing the best route and now jumping into the car, he looked out the windshields as he saw Violet standing patiently on the curb.

"Oh shit, I'm sorry. Let me help you in the car," he said sheepishly. "Okay, we're all set."

Violet inquired, "Where is my bag?"

Tony, now completely exasperated, said, "Oh Shit!" as he ran back inside to retrieve the case.

Tony jumped back in the car, turned the ignition but it didn't start. Someone forgot to plug up the charging unit the night before. Tony, Tony, Tony...

"SHIT!" yelled Tony.

"Now what are we going to do...Papa Dabb?" said Violet with as much restraint as she could muster.

"I have no fucking idea," said Tony as he hung his head in shame, tearing up in frustration.

"Look, I'm sorry. It will be okay. We just need to think," said Violet as she took Tony's hand.

"I know. I'll call Billy. He should be down at the marina, and he can maybe come get us," said Tony.

"Good idea. Try him."

Tony dialed. Billy answered. The phone went dead. It showed no service.

"Great! Now what!"

Then, they heard an unusual sound outside of the garage. It was the sound of a gas powered engine.

Peering out, they saw Marty wheel in, driving the old S-10.

"A little bird told me you guys might need my help. Not many people do these days, so I thought I would come see."

"Uncle Marty! You are a lifesaver."

"I've been called a lot of things in my life, but never a lifesaver."

"I don't know how you knew, but I have to get Violet to the hospital. She is contracting."

"Do you remember how to drive my truck? I told you, you never know when you're gonna need to know how to drive a truck."

"I think so. Why don't you come with us?"

"No, I think you two can handle it. I'll just keep an eye on the house...and the Blue Moons."

"Okay. Wish us luck."

And we were off, heading down Highway 70 toward Carteret General Birthing Center.

"I'd better call Dad and let him know that we are on our way," said Tony.

"Hi, Dad. Yes, everything's fine. Violet's having contractions and we are on our way to Morehead. No, nothing to worry about.

Just come on when you're ready. Call Billy and Elva and let them know. Okay, gotta go. Love ya."

Just then the gas indicator beeper went off, of course, it did.

"Shit!" said Tony.

"What now?"

"I gotta stop and get gas if I can find a place that has gas."

"Great," sighed Violet.

"It'll be okay. We are just outside of Newport, and I remember a convenience store on Chatham Street that still had a gas pump. I will turn up ahead and hope that it still does."

Pulling into the Newport Mini-Mart and seeing the gas pump, Violet said, "You pay, I'll pump."

She hopped out and started to fill the tank between contractions.

"Hello, little lady. Out of gas?"

Hearing a familiar sounding voice, she looked up to see Pastor Bob coming her way.

"I can't believe that worthless piece of shit husband of yours has you out here pumping gas in your condition. I would never allow a pretty little thing like you to do that. Let me help you pump it."

Looking straight into Bob's eyes, she glared at him and turned away without a word.

"Don't look away from me woman. Judgement day has finally come for you."

Violet reached up to touch Bob's forehead to alter his thoughts. As she did, she felt an incredible shock of pain in her right arm...and then a snap.

"Aargh..." shrieked Violet, as she grabbed her right arm. A dull pressure followed the sharp pain. Violet started throwing up. Luckily, the bone had not pierced the skin, but she felt extremely dizzy.

"Maybe that belly will pop just like your arm did," said Bob moving toward her with a knife. Pretty dumb trying to use those parlor tricks that Sopie did. They didn't stop me then, and they won't stop me now. Those twins will never be born," said the legion of voices from the evil inside the pastor.

Violet, who had shaken off her dizziness, said, "No, dumb is attacking someone with a gas hose in one hand and a zippo in the other," filling Pastor Bob's trousers with gasoline.

"Oh, and I'm not Sopie, Asshole," she said as she thumbed the wheel across the flint and tossed the lighter at the Celebrant. "Go to Hell."

Running, as best she could, she found shelter behind a nearby dumpster just as she saw Marty's beloved S-10 and the gas pumps explode from the kindling of the pastor.

"No…" yelled Tony running out of the store just in time to witness the ghastly scene of Pastor Bob experiencing the rapture as his ashes ascended skyward. He then remembered what he had stumbled across in Mark's memoirs when Master Bennie disclosed to Mark that the only way to truly defeat evil is through love and purification. You cannot defeat a force like this by fighting or killing the one possessed. The only way that the evil spirit can be stopped completely is to return it to the fourth dimension where it can be purified and hopefully rehabilitated. But it was too late. The demon within Pastor Bob had escaped and covered the entire area.

The sky turned dark filled with a putrid stench that smelled like the paper mills did before the EPA had shut all of those down. Tony looked frantically for Violet before he located her hunkering down by the dumpster.

"Are you alright?"

"Yes, but my arm is broken."

"We have got to get you to the hospital. Here…" handing Violet the phone, "call Dad and tell him where we are."

But before she could make the call, all Hell broke loose…literally.

Car after car started crashing into one another, people started fighting each other, first with fists and then, some pulled tire irons and baseball bats from their nearby vehicles.

A mini-Armageddon had begun.

"Hello. Violet?" said Amy.

"Yes, Momma B, it's me. We need your help. NOW," she cried uncontrollably, crouching behind the dumpster."

"Where are you? What's the matter?"

"I can't explain right now. We are at a convenience store in Newport on Chatham Street, and if we don't get help right away, we are not going to make it," said Violet sobbing.

"Not make it? What do you mean, not make it?"

"I mean we are going to die if you don't get us out of here."

"We are already on our way and almost to Newport. Just try to stay calm and stay on the phone with me. What the hell is going on? Where's Tony?"

"He's here hiding behind the dumpster with me."

"Why are you hiding behind a dumpster? What's happening?"

"People are rioting and fighting everywhere," cried Violet hysterically, "Just come get us!"

Jodi, Amy and I were about a half a mile from the Mini-Market when we hit the maelstrom.

The crowd of people, now consumed with the evil, began beating each other to death. Whipped into an uncontrollable frenzy, they started pummeling each other and anyone else that got in their way. Women and children were not spared as bones snapped and heads were crushed. Chatham Street quickly transformed into a river of blood as the survivors began looting Newport Garden Center, grabbing axes, shovels, sledgehammers and any other implement that they could get their hands on. Soon they were working their way toward the spot where Violet and Tony were hiding.

The convenience store owner came out and confronted the crowd, but was quickly knocked off his feet by a strike to the head with a baseball bat rendering him unconscious, lying in a pool of his own blood.

As the crowd moved toward the dumpster, Tony quickly responded, throwing kicks and punches at the oncoming horde.

"Tony DON'T!" shrieked Violet.

But Tony ignored her warning as he began dispatching his adversaries one by one as quickly as they rushed in. As two or more came at him, he would disappear and reappear behind them quickly subduing them before they knew what hit them. But even with Tony's superlative combat skills coupled with inter-dimensional evasion, he was not able to repel the crowd without injuries. A searing pain struck his left shoulder as it was grazed with an ax, creating a gaping wound pouring blood down his arm and fingers.

"Tony!" Violet shrieked.

"Stay back!" yelled Tony, just as he took the ax from his attacker and returned it deep in his skull. Then he heard the pump...of a shotgun. But before the assailant could get off the shot, Tony flipped the gun back toward him discharging the weapon causing his corpse to blow back into two more vigilantes as they fell to the pavement.

He had fought before, yes...but never so many attackers at one time. It would have been an effort in futility for anyone else, but his training and his love for Violet and the twins kept him going. Ignoring the seething pain in his shoulder, he relentlessly defeated one opponent after another in what appeared to be a replay of the Alamo. They just kept coming.

I wheeled my car into the parking lot, running over three of the men yelling, "Get in!"

Jodi jumped out of the car and began to help ward off the frenzied crowd as she joined Tony in the fight.

I again yelled, "Get in the car!"

Jodi helped a hysterical Violet stumble to the car and got her in. Then Jodi got Violet to focus and said to her, "Open a portal...NOW!"

Violet did as instructed, just as Jodi was pulled from the car by a shovel-wielding moron that quickly dug his own grave.

The sky suddenly turned a bright magenta, and hurricane force winds started to swirl creating a vortex that got larger and larger as it turned on its side. Lightning lit up the sky as the portal appeared.

Jodi grabbed Tony's face with both hands, staring him in the eyes, "Leave me. Violet needs you. I've got this. You know this is my fight, not yours. I've been preparing for this day my whole life. I love you guys, now GO!"

Tony, begrudgingly, entered the SUV as Jodi continued with the fight. I spun out heading toward the hospital, carrying the bloody duo as Violet's water broke.

"Oh, God!"

Tony said calmly, "Breathe," as he tried his best to recall the Lamaze techniques they had learned.

I said, "Try to calm yourself. Don't worry. I will have you two at the hospital in 15 minutes."

"Be careful," said Amy, "there is construction on the road ahead!"

So I veered to the left and took Bridges Street off of Arendell, which runs behind the hospital. Whipping under the canopy of the emergency room, I jumped out.

"Hey, we need some help out here!"

As Jodi turned away from the car, she heard a loud CRACK! She felt her flesh tear from her face. Two ranchers then began to flog her bullwhips. She fell to the ground as her adversaries kept striking. Withstanding excruciating pain, Jodi somehow managed to regain her footing between strikes and grab one of the whips and returned the favor. As she knocked one of the men out with a back kick, the other had pulled a strand of barbed wire from his pickup and ran toward her in an attempt to strangle her. However, she squatted into a horse stance to avoid it catching her throat. Unfortunately, it wrapped around her skull and sank deep in her forehead. The blood trickled down her face and into her eyes. She could taste the salt from the sweat and the blood...her blood.

Jodi lashed out blindly with a final fury of kicks that finished off the last attacker. Then with outstretched arms, she said, "It is Finished...Take Me," as she stumbled toward the portal.

The evil pierced her side and entered in. It attempted to destroy her spirit, but the light from the unconditional love that she held inside her heart overshadowed the evil and began to consume it. As she entered the portal, Jodi said, "Father, I entrust my spirit into your hands." And then the real battle began...

Epiphany

---

*L*ight always shines greyest when you can't seem to make sense of the world, when what you're seeing just can't be true. Jodi now found herself in a very different place. There was no light. There was no dark. There was nothing except void. There was no sound, no smell, no sensation whatsoever. A nothingness that was both haunting and yet somehow comforting. There was light above. She could see it. There was darkness down below. She could feel it. The love inside her was still there. Brilliant, but hidden. Trying to force its way up toward the light. The evil was still inside her as well, trying to release itself from the overwhelming power of the love. It was sinking to the bottom and the love rising to the top pulling Jodi in both directions. She had no choice but to allow one to escape. It would be an easy choice for anyone except Jodi, who believed there was always hope in all things. And it was this hope that made the love eventually pull her up and the evil sink down, down into the abyss.

When she reached the top of the nothingness, there was a great opening of light.

VIOLET HASTILY WAS WHEELED into the emergency room at Carteret General. The twins were definitely on their way, but the medical team needed to get her stabilized before she headed to the birthing center.

Amy, Tony and I just sat and waited outside of the emergency room, after Tony gave the nurse in the admission's office the required medical and insurance information. One of the med-techs said that her obstetrician, Dr. Hamlisch, was on his way and should arrive in about twenty minutes. In the meantime, they were going to attend to her broken arm and place an immobilizer on it.

As they did, she had another contraction.

"Breathe, Honey," said Tony.

"Breathe my ass," screamed Violet as she farted. "Oops! Sorry."

"It's okay," said Tony bleeding and smiling, but concerned. "Everything is going to be alright. Just breathe."

"Riggs..."

"Don't even say it," said Tony, "don't even say it."

Billy and Elva arrived about 15 minutes later and joined us in the waiting area outside the emergency room. Both had looks of concern and confusion on their faces.

"What's happened to the kids? Why are they in the emergency room and not the birthing center?" asked Billy.

"It's a long story, Dad. There was some kind of a riot in Newport when the kids stopped to get gas. It was horrible. We were able to get them in the car. Violet, I think has a broken arm and Tony has some wounds, but I think they both will be okay," sighed Amy.

"I don't quite understand. Why did they need gas?" said Billy.

"I think, from what they said, the car's battery was dead, and they used Uncle Marty's truck to drive to the hospital, but it was low on fuel."

"Where's Jodi? Wasn't she riding with you?" asked Elva.

Amy teared up, unable to speak.

I continued, "We had no choice but to leave Jodi in Newport. After getting Violet and Tony in the car, she refused to leave. She left us no choice but to leave her behind so we could save the babies." I said, now also breaking down, crying uncontrollably, "How will I ever be able to explain that to Gabriel and Seneca."

Billy and Elva just sat there in shock. They could not comprehend the horror of the situation that we had just witnessed.

Finally, Billy stood up, went over to me and hugged me saying, "It's going to be alright. I know you did all that you could do." Reflecting on his time as a young man serving in the military in Afghanistan, he continued, "Decisions like that are tough...very tough, but you had to make the one that would save the most lives."

The medical team assumed that our battered and bleeding kids had been in a car accident on their way to the hospital until ambulance after ambulance started to arrive from Newport turning the triage unit into a 36-hour marathon of MASH reruns. The nurses kept trying to attend to Tony, but he refused. He was not leaving Violet's side.

A few minutes later, Dr. Hamlisch did arrive. He re-examined Violet's arm and had it X-rayed again, but was surprised to find no signs of a break. All Violet and Tony seemed to have, were superficial cuts and bruises. He then had the couple escorted to the delivery and birthing center. Everyone else followed the couple to the delivery waiting room.

Examining Violet's cervix, he found a full dilation of 10 cm and then a crowning of the first baby.

"When I tell you, push, but not before."

"Okay," Violet panted.

"Now, push," he said.

And she did.

"Once more, push."

And little boy Banos was born with a single cry.

A nurse laid him on the table as the doctor prepared to receive the second child.

"Push harder."

And Violet pushed.

"Once more," he said as he extracted the little girl.

Violet smiling said, "Are they both okay?"

"Absolutely," the doctor said as the nurse laid both children on her breasts.

"This is unbelievable. It's an absolute miracle," said Tony.

"Yes, Tony. It's a miracle," Violet said, as the new parents stared in awe at the twins.

"Well, I guess now I will be able to teach them how to sail and fish and...drink scotch!"

"Oh, I don't think you will have to teach at least one of them how to drink scotch. But they are here to teach us...remember."

"Oh, that right. I almost forgot about that part," said Tony. "I wonder what our mission will be."

"Oh shit, I forgot about that part, too. Didn't we just complete our mission?"

"No, that was Jodi's mission. God bless her," looking down at the floor."

Looking up, Tony asked, "Did you just burp?"

"No, I don't think so," said Violet.

All of a sudden, Violet had a sudden sharp pain in her abdomen. The doctor went in to re-examine her again, fearing a hemorrhage.

As JODI FLOATED UPWARD toward the great light, she found herself landing on a sunny beach. In total disbelief, she began to look around in all directions, acclimating herself to her new surroundings. She could feel the warmth of the sun on her face. She could smell the salt air and feel the gentle breeze blowing.

Jodi began walking down the beach, listening to the seagulls. A few steps farther she finds a starfish and tosses it back into the ocean. This just had to be heaven, of course, it was.

A voice behind her disrupted her reverie, "Welcome home."

She turned to see an older man putting up beach umbrellas and chairs.

"Hi, I'm Melvin, the caretaker."

"Pleased to meet you," said Jodi.

"Better not keep the old man waiting. HE's expecting you," said Melvin pointing to what looked like a resort up ahead.

Not asking questions, Jodi moved toward the building.

Upon arriving at the entrance, the doors swung open as a valet said, "Come in. We've been expecting you. Go down this hallway to the last door on the right. HE's waiting for you."

"Thank you," said Jodi as she continued nervously down the hallway.

She reached the door and started to knock when the door opened. Hesitantly, she entered finding herself inside a room, a very comfortable place that wrapped itself around her.

"Hello Jodisan," said a voice.

"Are you...?"

"I AM. You have done very well, my little cherub," as his form then changed to that of Sister Amyra.

"You have fulfilled your mission, my child, by eliminating the threat to the twins and by delivering the evil to the lower fourth dimension. It is there that we may be able to rehabilitate his soul, thanks to your unconditional love and sacrifice."

"I knew from the beginning that I had to give up my life so that the twins could be born again," said Jodi, a little sadly.

Amyra now changed her form once again, and Uncle Marty stood before her.

Marty said, "But only for a short while. Wouldn't you like to join the twins?"

"Yes, of course, I would! But how would that be possible?"

"All things are possible with...well, you know. Arise and go. Return to guard Heaven's gate once more," pointing toward the light. "I will see you later then?" He said, sipping his Blue Moon letting out a loud belch.

As she arose and headed toward the top of the light, she heard, "Push! Once more. There is a third child! Another girl!"

And so it begins...

"And in the beginning...

God saw everything that he had made, and, it was very good."

Thank you for taking the time to read "Sonny's Boy." If you enjoyed it, please consider telling your friends or posting a short review. Word of mouth is an author's best friend and much appreciated.

About the Author

"Spencer Michaels" is the pen name of the father-son writing team comprised of Michael and Spencer Bennington. When friends ask how the collaboration began, son Spencer is quick to joke that his dad, Michael, guilted him into becoming a writing partner. That wry sense of humor smacks of modesty as Spencer is also an Adjunct Professor of English and a doctoral student at the University of South Florida and works as a freelance writer. In addition, he is an accomplished Tae Kwon Do instructor.

One might say that entertaining is in Michael Bennington's blood. Prior to becoming a novelist, he worked as a professional musician for over 50 years playing varied venues from night clubs to coliseums and even recorded CDs and served as back up to nationally known recording artists. He shared his love of music as a teacher at Sacred Heart Catholic School for 13 years before retiring in 2012. He says that these days his music is limited to playing at his church where he serves as choir director.

Besides their son Spencer, Michael and Susie, have one other son, Miki, two grandchildren, Tyler and Kayla and a Sheltie named Luci, who the family considers their only daughter.

Stay in touch with Spencer Michaels here…

f facebook.com/spencermichaelsbooks

y twitter.com/SMichaelsBooks

p pinterest.com/SpencerMichaelsBooks